# FIRE HORSE

*Obsession never dies*

*a novel by*

**KATE LE PAGE**

***For Frank, Amanda & David***

***Illustration: K. Kivlichan***

*comments:* *kkfire1969@gmail.com*

*Any resemblance to people or animals, living or deceased, is purely coincidental, with the exception of Lizzie, "a real Beagle."*

## *AUTHOR'S NOTE*

"Fire Horse" was put together and written in Scotland, England and the USA, both at home and on my travels. It is an idea based on a series of stories written between 1981 and 84. The plot and some of the characters are based on this.

Although not autobiographical as such, some ideas and incidents were taken from my own youth. Anyone who knows me well should be able to untangle fact from fiction...and wishful thinking!

Like Helen, I longed for a horse when I was young, so I invented some with my friends and had many good times pretending to ride them! I enjoyed drawing pictures of them and giving them characteristics. Some of these horses are in this story!

This is purely a tale for enjoyment, although it is also intended as a nostalgia trip for those of us who remember the days of furry dice and leg warmers!

I wish to thank my family and dear friends, including the animals in my life over the years who have helped me, supported me and inspired me (or just nagged me) to "keep on keeping on." Please enjoy, as this one is on me!

*June 2019*

# CHAPTER ONE

*1984*

Rain trickled down the window as I sat at my desk enduring a double period of mathematics, just wishing that the time would pass. Even the view from the third floor window looked tired and worn, as if it too had had enough of foul weather and double maths. Normally the upper windows of Braepark High School gave onto a peaceful view of rolling green fields dotted with peacefully grazing cattle, but today it was shrouded in a gloomy mist. I had considered, hopefully, that there may be something wrong with my watch and it was in fact later than this. Adults often warned me that in so doing, I was wishing my life away, and that when I was older I would want things to slow down just a little to avoid old age arriving too quickly. However, at fourteen, old age was something which simply happened to other people, not to me. Anything which prolonged the school day after all, could not be good by anyone's standards!

"Thank goodness that's over! That was one of the longest days ever!" my best friend Jessica remarked as we splashed through the puddles of the school playground, making our way to the waiting school bus which would have us back home in around twenty minutes, outside our favourite newsagents' shop. We would pick up just enough sweets to keep us going but not enough to put us off our dinner.

This was a big treat for us and we really looked forward to the end of the school day. Having endured a whole day of school at this level when we were working towards our main exams was really something. We deserved a rest and we also deserved the sweets. Our evenings were of course supposed to be spent doing homework and revision. We did our share it has to be said, but it was not our main concern. I maybe should have more shame in saying that, but I do not!

Jess and I had been friends since our first day of primary school. She was easy going and caring and I felt really lucky to have her as my best friend. Of course she was cleverer and better looking than me, or at least I thought so. Jess kept telling me I was lovely and that I should have more confidence in myself. That was what I loved about her.

Jessica's parents were well off, much better off than mine, due to having their own haulage company which was not far from their home. I did not complain as I was loved and cared for. Jess, however, lived on the outskirts of town, just a ten minute walk from my own home. They were fortunate enough to have a small holding called One Tree Farm, and this was where Jess and I indulged in our one common passion – horses. Jess had a horse of her own, a pretty mare named Mary Rose who was rather handy in the show jumping ring. I did not own a horse. My parents simply did not have the money for it and even when I was young, I had this explained to me and was not down-hearted. Born an optimist, I made the most. I helped around their yard as they had other horses, some of which I could ride as and when I wished. I knew I was more fortunate than many people and in some ways I knew how to make my own luck. I did get down-hearted at times but knew from experience not to let it ground me for too long.

Jess's father had an interesting sideline. He bought horses every so often which he worked with and then sold on when he felt they had been re-attuned as it were. He had many contacts and was often tipped off about a horse or pony in need of rescue. However, no horse or pony was ever sold until Roger Brookes was one hundred per cent sure that he or she was fit, healthy and ready to be moved on. He also made sure that any potential owner was aware of what they were taking on and knew how to look after them. It was vital that these often mistreated animals did not face any more hardship. Many came to him as "problem horses" in quite a sorry state, and he was what would come to be known as a "horse whisperer." These horses often came described as "misfits" and sometimes I thought of myself that way too.

It happened fairly often, and seemed unfair. People with the means but no skills acquired horses who turned out to be totally unsuitable and so many ended up being flogged in auction rings or just abandoned, many in a miserable condition. Yet there were people like me at the other end of the scale, willing to put in all the hours of hard work in any weather, but without the means. However, there was always something of interest for me. Jess's father's sideline often involved both of us in the re-training of some of the horses and ponies he had acquired. It was through this that I was secretly hoping my luck would change and I may be able to somehow own a horse or pony which had come to Jess's father's yard for this reason. However, in order to be able to actually purchase a horse I would need a miracle and I knew it. At just fourteen I was in no position to earn the money I needed for this purpose. I was a dreamer but also a realist at the end of the day. I knew that I just had to carry on making the most.

For a while now, a horse called Heidi had been resident at One Tree Farm. She was the kind of horse I dreamed of as my ideal mount. She was a neat and compact bay mare who was about eleven years old and didn't require a great deal of training. Her previous owner had simply fallen on hard times and needed to sell up and move on. I often sat in my untidy, cramped bedroom drawing pictures of Heidi when I was meant to be studying. I dreamed of owning her, of doing well in the show ring and having my name in the local papers or, better still, on TV….

"I know you love Heidi" Jess's father had remarked one day as I finished exercising her, "But don't get too attached because if someone comes along and gives me an offer, I'll need to take it. It's how we work around here, Helen. We all get fond of them when they've been here a while but we just can't keep everyone. I'm saying this because I don't want to see you upset again. It's not just the money, it's the time. We'd be overwhelmed if we had to look after all of them every day."

“I know” I sighed, patting Heidi’s neck, “It was the same with Beauty if you remember. I really liked him but that girl who bought him was ideal for him and she really loved him. I’m used to it, really I am. I just want to help so that these horses can move on to the homes they deserve.” I said that more to convince myself than Roger Brookes, however. Deep down I really, really wanted a horse to call my own and give all my care and attention to. I was allowed to ride Buster and Minx any time I wanted, but to be fair their best years were behind them. They were pets more than anything else, quiet companion horses for Mary Rose and for any of the other horses and ponies who spent time there.

“I hope this rain goes off!” Jess interrupted my daydreams of Heidi as she tore at the paper on her sticky toffee with her teeth on our way back to her place under the flimsy shelter of my old umbrella, “I was hoping we could get the jumps out tonight and get Mary and Heidi over them.”

“Me too” I sighed, “We deserve a bit of a giggle after double maths, and having to listen to Samantha Inglis going on and on about how much money she has!”

“Oh, let’s not talk about her!” groaned Jess, “When she was going on about her Dad and his speed boat and all that I started wishing it would sink with her in it, just to fill up her mouth and stop her talking if nothing else!” We looked at each other and both giggled through our mouthfuls of sweets, at this hideous image of the designer-clad school know-all soaked through with a mouthful of seaweed!

We both had homework but instead of doing it, we ended up listening to music in Jess's room while flicking through pop magazines and laughing over some of the comments made at school during the day. There was a tale about a teacher using leg warmers to fix his car exhaust and this was still causing some mirth. We were very relieved to see the rain had finally gone off and a watery sun was making an appearance as the clouds slowly receded.

"I don't think we can jump too high with the ground this muddy" said Jess and I had to agree. I hadn't been able to go round for a few days now due to family visiting and studying for a French test which was now behind me, so I was looking forward to seeing the horses again. One Tree Farm (which was actually full of trees) was a lovely and relaxing place, and the yard was kept very neat and clean. Sometimes I dreamed that my own family home was like this, rather than the modest and slightly shabby terraced house we lived in. But it was home and I loved it.

Heidi was happy to see me as always, as was the Brookes family's dog, a bouncy, exuberant Beagle named Lizzie. Before I went and got Heidi's saddle and bridle, I glanced at the next 3 stables to see if there were any new horses or ponies in. The first stable was empty but a small grey pony came up to me in the second one, sticking his head over the door and nibbling cheekily at my pockets in search of any food I may be harbouring. I grinned and told him,

"Sorry, I didn't bring any today! I'll try and remember next time." There was also a new horse next to Heidi, a large chestnut which I hadn't seen before either. He had mud on his sparse coat and a few ribs showing. This was clearly a horse who needed some work done on him. I checked the door, but as yet no temporary name sticker had appeared, just the same as the grey pony. The horses who lived here had permanent wooden plaques bearing their names, but the transitory ones only had an identification sticker on their door until they moved on. As I got Heidi ready for my ride, the chestnut horse took an interest in me, pushing his nose against the wooden slats to try and get my attention. He managed to find a space large enough to get through to me and I held my hand out to let him sniff and then lick it. He had a kind, friendly eye but he showed signs of neglect, which was always sad to see. His fiery red mane was long and tangled from neglect and his coat was dull and staring. I have always believed that animals deserve love and kindness. As I always did, I just hoped this horse would be able to find his forever home as soon as possible. His coat really was a stunning shade of rusty bronze – Flame? Firestorm? Blaze, maybe? I knew that Jess's father would do his utmost to rehabilitate the chestnut horse and grey pony to the best of his abilities.

Jess and I made the most of what we had but with the ground being wet from all the rain, we had to keep the jumps fairly low and be cautious. A slip could cause them both to be injured, and us too of course. However, we never considered ourselves in the same way as we did the horses. We always just assumed we would bounce back if we hurt ourselves. We didn't want to hurt the horses through our own recklessness, though. As it was, we came away laughing as we always did, covered in the mud which had splashed up onto us as we rode round our course of jumps. My parents were used to this now, and tended to just shrug when I came in covered in mud from top to toe. They did not complain when I deposited a pile of muddy clothing in the basket next to our decidedly unreliable washing machine, alongside my brother Richard's filthy overalls from the garage. They really did have to put up with quite a lot!

"Have you thought any more about what you want to do when you leave school?" my father asked later that evening as we were finishing supper. He had been unlucky in his own line of work as a ship builder, so he had real concern on his face every time he asked me this. He put his cup of coffee down which always meant he was serious. Career choice was a very common question in this household and I really felt that they wanted me to change my mind!

"I really want to work with horses." It may not have been the most practical of replies, but my heart was set on it.

"I know how much you love them, Helen" my father reasoned, "But you need to try and think of the future, although I know that's hard. It's a lot of work, long hours for very little pay and it isn't the most secure either. You might be better with a back up plan, just in case. You've got a good brain and you may be better with a career where you could earn enough money to be able to still keep up your interest in horses. Please don't be mad at me, I don't want to lecture you. Things don't always work out as you expect, no matter how hard you try. I'm just saying, there are other options."

"I know, I know. I do all my homework and you've seen my report card." I sighed, "But it's just that I can't see myself sitting in an office all dressed up, not a mud puddle in sight! It really isn't me, Dad." That and the fact I'm hopeless at maths, I found myself thinking.

"I know that, but I'm just trying to point out that sometimes in life we have to do things we don't want to do, to get to our dreams. I don't want to put you off if your heart's set on that. All work doesn't need to be office based, there are other things you could do. And no, I'm not going to say *when I was your age* because I know it won't cut any ice with you, and I won't compare you to other girls or your brother."

I smiled to myself. I did listen and tried to take on board all the advice from my parents. I was not perfect and we did argue at times, simply because I felt they really didn't understand how I felt about horses. They also didn't understand what it was like to be young in the 1980's. However, I knew they had lived and not everything was easy for them, especially as my father had problems with employment since his job at the ship yard had ended abruptly, and my mother had little choice but to stay at home taking care of us. In fact she'd had to abandon a university course for that reason. But I was a born dreamer and if I'm honest, a misfit. I knew more than most people that horse work was not glamorous, easy or well paid. In fact, a great deal of the work was cleaning up, scrubbing, and working out of doors for long hours in all types of weather, all year round. Injuries were common as it was very physically demanding. Nevertheless, at that moment in time, all I wanted in my life was to be with horses and I was prepared to move heaven and earth if necessary, just to achieve that goal.

## CHAPTER TWO

For a few weeks not much riding or horse work was done, as we had some mock exams and my parents told me that no matter what job I was planning, it would be better for me to do well at my academic subjects so that I had them to fall back on. I was glad that I listened to my parents as I knew they were right about that, although my mind still wandered from my books and I dreamed of galloping Heidi through the woods with the wind in my hair. I still doodled and scribbled, drawing little miniature pictures of Heidi on the paper I was using to take notes. It was better to have something to back me up should things not go according to plan. But at times I did feel guilty about my wandering mind, not paying attention and then suddenly jumping back to reality when I realised a teacher was speaking directly to me. Leaving school early with no qualifications would give me fewer options and I knew it. Maybe horse work did not require academic prowess, but not giving it my best shot would give me less flexibility. My parents were right about this and I knew it, but it didn't stop me from dreaming.

All the time that I was battling with my exams, my eyes drifted to the skyline outside the school window, leading me beyond the drudgery of the classroom and out to the yard and the fields where Jess and I would spend our upcoming summer holidays riding and working with the horses as much as we could. My parents could not afford holidays and I accepted that, so being at the yard was a great comfort to me. I didn't really care about the lack of holidays; I loved to lie on my back on a warm, sunny day beneath the trees with Jess. Side by side we'd talk over our hopes and dreams for the future with the blades of grass stirring gently in the breeze while the horses grazed peacefully in the fields.

"You know there's no money in horse work" declared Samantha Inglis as we rode home on the school bus the day after the final exam, "My mum says you work 16 hours a day for about fifteen pounds a week!" I tried not to let my anger get the better of me. Samantha was one of those people who thought she knew everything, or at least thought her mother did. She knew nothing about horses anyway, and I thought she may be jealous because Jess and I had such a good friendship and were so focussed on the horses and what we wanted to do. As Jess pointed out, Samantha's parents were well off and she was going out with Peter Radcliffe, a boy whom many girls wouldn't mind dating. If she was so happy in herself, why would she need to hit on us for liking horses so much? We both reckoned it was to do with her parents, both of them university lecturers, and the fact that her older sister had been accepted for Edinburgh University. Naturally, everyone in town knew about this…

Boys. A subject that, at the age of fourteen, I was apparently supposed to be very interested in. However, I had discovered a long time ago that I was not the conventional child, not the textbook copy which some parents hoped for. Luckily for me, though, my parents were not either. None of us bothered particularly with convention, especially as my father's lifelong career as a shipbuilder was now over due to mass redundancies at yards up and down the country. Getting married and producing grandchildren seemed to be no more on their agenda than it was on mine. In the most innocent sense of the word, I preferred older men. My brother Richard's friends were often around and, as he was eighteen, some of them were already working. Andy, who was an apprentice garage mechanic, was very chatty and down to earth but even then, there were no romantic feelings. We all just had a laugh, the same as some of the people who came and went working at Jess's father's haulage yard, which was half a mile or so from their smallholding. I even chatted and joked with Terry, the school bus driver but it was all just a big laugh to us.

If anyone mentioned marriage and children, we just laughed it off as we were too young to be worried about that at this stage in life. Exams seemed to loom larger than anything, followed by the pressure of getting into college or university, or getting a job. Guys were just guys and in all honesty, most of those in my own year group were so immature that it was a miracle to me that they had even made it through primary school. The few I did like were just good friends, people I talked to. I had to face the fact that no man in his right mind was ever going to fancy me. Helen Doyle, the muddy, bedraggled dreamer, frequently late for school, falling over her shoe laces, no make up, no hair do, not to mention flat-chested. Posters in magazines depicted perfectly turned out females in suits, with smart, neat hair, perfect figures, immaculate jewellery and absolutely no dirt under their exquisitely manicured nails. I saw myself as plain, too small, too thin with wispy light brown hair and one or two stray freckles. No figure to speak of.

Girls like Samantha definitely looked down on me but I didn't care. I had realised a while ago that people liked me and they were the ones who counted, not those who judged by my appearance or how much money my parents did or did not earn. I was definitely not the most confident of people but I still had enough self-assurance to be myself and follow my own dreams. I didn't feel the need to do certain things just because my peers were doing them.

With the exams finally behind us, I was glad to get back to the normality of Jess's father's yard. It was near the end of the school term now, no more serious work and not many days to go.

"Oh by the way" said Jess, as we ditched our school bags in her back porch and went to get changed into our riding gear, "Dad managed to sell that grey pony Smoky. Wasn't here for long but there was a kid we knew for some years and his pony had died not long ago. Just fell in love with Smoky right away regardless of what training he has or hasn't had. Had just the one ride on him and that was that."

"Great" I said, "Has he any new ones in?"

"Yes, there's a new mare who's really skittish, terrified of everything, makes us wonder what on earth happened to her. Oh and the big chestnut's still with us. His name's Barney. Anyway, he's going to be a handful so it looks like 2 problem ones for now. They wouldn't deliberately hurt you, but being on their backs could be something else. Not sure either of them would be like Heidi. In fact I'm surprised no one's put in an offer for her yet!" I felt a cold, uneasy tightening in the pit of my stomach whenever this was mentioned. Despite my best intentions and all the warnings from Roger Brookes, I had indeed fallen for Heidi. I knew she was not and would never be mine but I couldn't help it. She'd now been on the yard for nearly 6 months and that was more than long enough for me to fall in love. I kept it quiet but knew by the way Jess looked at me that the penny had dropped with her some time ago. It would just remain unspoken for now. It was probably the biggest thing that set me apart from Jess, or at least in some people's reckoning. They had money, we did not. We both knew deep down that I may never be able to afford what I really wanted. I didn't mind when she went on skiing holidays or told me about her first class travel to the Walt Disney parks in Orlando. I just wanted a horse.

Down at the yard, while I was getting Heidi ready for a ride in the woods, the chestnut horse next door spotted me again and stuck his head through the wooden slats to have a good look at me. Barney. This time I had remembered the carrot slices and quickly fed him a few. The horse took them happily. He looked slightly better now. He was still on the thin side but his coat looked better already. The dull, dusty appearance had been replaced by one of shining red-gold, and his full mane and tail were the colour of fire. If he was my horse, I would call him Flame, Rusty, Sunset or Wildfire, I thought, but

Barney? I would never have thought of that. He was a very big horse, too big and strong for a skinny teenager like myself to handle but I could dream. This was me, this was what I should be doing, I resolved. I should be admiring horses and taking in their good qualities, not thinking about guys who I had no chance at all of being with. What a waste of time that would be! I just hoped that Barney would grow in strength and one day be happy with a new owner. I always wondered what the horses' stories were, and hoped deep down that nothing too brutal had befallen them in their past lives.

Once I had finished my ride on Heidi, I went and checked on the new mare who Jess had told me about. She was a sorry sight, huddled in the far corner of her stable, looking terrified of everything and everyone. She was thin too, her ribs showing and her backbone protruding slightly. I glanced but as yet no temporary name sticker. I felt angry suddenly. Two more horses at the yard, two more who should have been loved and taken care of from the start. Now both needed to be properly fed and to have their various issues ironed out before they could start the long journey to the new life which they both so richly deserved. At least Smoky the pony had gone now, so there was hope.

Finally the last day of school was over. We got out early and the school buses came earlier than usual to deliver us to our beloved sweet shop. Everyone was in high spirits, people listening to music on headphones and ghetto blasters, happy because they were allowed to wear silly clothes and shoes on the final days of term, and no work was being done anyway.

I was so excited to be going home that I almost lost my footing and stumbled as I literally threw myself aboard the waiting school bus. Regaining my composure, I gingerly pulled myself upright, and found myself staring into the concerned, freckled face of Terry the bus driver.

"You OK, Helen?" he asked me, "Don't break any bones on your last day or you'll have rubbish school holidays!"

"Too right!" I laughed, "But it'll be rubbish anyway, not seeing you!"

"So, do you want to put the wedding invites on ice for a while then?"

"Yeah Terry, you're miles too old for me. I don't want to be pushing you around in a bath chair when I'm still in my 30's!"

"Cheek!" said Terry, "I'm not *that* much older than you!" He winked at me, which made me giggle. He was actually a very good looking man with his riot of sandy blond hair and a neat sprinkling of freckles across the bridge of his nose. His blue eyes twinkled when he smiled. Why had I just realised this now, I wondered? I'd known Terry since I was twelve!

"It's OK, Terry, Helen always said she wanted to work with the elderly!" Jess jokingly snapped me out of my daydreams as she got on behind me, "I seem to have lost my bus fare again!"

"Who cares?" I grinned, "I never pay my fare and anyway, we're off school for 6 weeks!"

So here we were. Six weeks of spending as much time as possible at the stables, helping out, riding the horses, helping where we could with the new ones and just generally having a laugh, listening to pop music and enjoying our freedom. Bliss!

When I returned home, however, my parents were both sitting in the living room with no TV or music on, which was not at all like them. I knew something was wrong straight away.

"Helen" said my mother, steering me towards the sofa and sitting me down, "Your aunt Jean in Aberdeen's had a stroke. She's going to be OK hopefully but we'll need to go up there and stay for about 3 weeks, then Lesley and Colin will take over. I know you had a lot of plans with Jess and the horses but you'll have to do that later in the holidays now. It just can't be helped."

I didn't know what to say, as I gazed helplessly out of the window into the street. I was very fond of my great aunt Jean and very sorry that she wasn't well. We'd had some great times together in the past and it was only right that we went and did our share. My aunt was unmarried with no family of her own so it was fitting that the rest of us shared out the responsibilities.

“Can’t I stay with Jess or something? I’d pay my way, I’d work at the yard every day!” I pleaded, feeling guilty even as I said it. My parents were quiet for a bit, and even looked at each other as if considering that, raising my hopes slightly.

“It’s not about you staying with Jess because I don’t think her parents would refuse especially if you were working but 3 weeks is quite a long time and Aunt Jean’s family. She likes you and she’d wonder where you were. In fact, you’re a breath of fresh air for her, she’s told us that. We’re kind of hoping that you being there might help her a bit, might make her feel a bit more upbeat. I’m really sorry, Helen, I know you’ve been looking forward to this, and you’ve worked really hard and deserve your time off” my mother eventually told me, “But you have to see it from our point of view too. It’s a family thing.”

I conceded as I had no choice, but I ended up feeling humiliated and even angry, then I felt guilty for even trying to wriggle out of it but it just wasn’t to be. Three weeks seemed interminable and so much could happen during that time. My beloved Heidi could be sold right under my nose with no chance to even say goodbye, and there was not one single thing I could do about it.

## CHAPTER THREE

The time seemed to drag. I had half hoped, with feelings of guilt, that our ancient Ford Cortina might be unable to make the trip up north, but somehow it got us there. The journey seemed interminable and the white furry dice in the front window seemed to mock me as they swung rhythmically to and fro, as if they were involved in a conspiracy with the car and my parents, to whisk me away from my ideal summer dream. My parents spent a lot of time running errands for my aunt who was bed-ridden and there were constant visitors in the form of nurses, doctors, neighbours, church visitors and a few others. I felt angry at times but hated myself for it so had to fight back those feelings. I had worked very hard this year and got through all my exams, and more than ever I had been looking forward to this summer break...But then my anger would turn back to guilt for even thinking this way.

"Chin up, Helen!" my father looked at me almost apologetically as I sprawled on the sofa with yet another novel, "I know it's hard, love, and I know how much you miss Jess and the horses, but it's just the way it is. We'll be home again before you know it."

I had brought plenty of books and also my diary in which I recorded both happenings and my own thoughts, and I managed to get a few walks when I was not running to and fro helping my parents with various things. We were lucky that there were some good places to walk in the area and I could take some time out to be alone with my thoughts and feelings while breathing the cool, northern air. My brother Richard arrived a little later on and I was again envious of him due to the fact that he was an adult which meant he didn't have to go everywhere our parents went, like I did. I appreciated the stability of home, having someone to do my washing and put my food on the table, but there was a part of me which craved freedom and independence. I thought of my brother and his friends, my friends' parents and even Terry. They had jobs which were a bit of a bind, but on the other hand they called the shots on their own lives. They didn't have someone telling them to do homework, tidy their room or visit their sick aunt, did they?

I managed to communicate with my aunt and it was almost like old times when she was able to talk with difficulty but she was weak and could only speak for a short time, feeling drained after her stroke. I felt eternally guilty as I secretly wished the time away, just as I had been advised not to do, until I could be back to my normal life. It may not be lavish or glamorous, but it was home and I loved it. I loved spending the time with Jess and her family, as well as my own family of course, but I preferred it when I could come and go and do my own thing, as it were. Aunt Jean didn't have any pets, not even a budgie, so I had no animal contact except with next door's elderly black and white cat who was not always in the mood for a cuddle and often looked at me disdainfully when I tried.

As if to mock my predicament, the sun shone relentlessly for most of the time that we spent with my aunt. In fact when we'd had an extremely warm Easter, many had said pessimistically that we'd had our summer. However, it was getting so hot now that there was talk of records being broken, and even some parts of the country suffering from drought and hosepipe bans.

I wrote Jess several letters but she, by her own admission, was not a great letter writer. I did receive one letter to the four I sent her, but in it she just wrote something about her sister having friends round and how annoying they had been. She had mentioned the horses briefly, saying nothing much had changed. At least that must mean Heidi was still with them, and I'd get to see her and ride her again.

When the day finally came for me to get back to the yard and see Jess and the horses, the typical British summer weather decided to do its worst. I shrugged on my waterproofs and Wellingtons amid distant protestations from my parents about "catching my death." Right at that moment I couldn't have cared less what I caught!

When I arrived at One Tree Farm, I was greeted by the sight of the 2 newest horses standing in the covered part of the yard. Mr Yardley the vet was having a look at the bay mare and he obviously had his work cut out. If he so much as raised his hand, she cowered away, her ears laid back and her eyes rolling, showing white. She was clearly very wound up for no apparent reason.

"She seems in good condition otherwise, Roger, but she's so nervous it's hard even to look her over without someone getting hurt. I want to leave her until she's a bit calmer but she's getting there. She'll need some work. I could sedate her but that's obviously an extreme step. If she needed any serious work done on her I'd have no option. But we won't stress her out any more for now." He was putting his instruments away in his bag and for the first time I got my first decent look at the mare. She was a very dark colour, like mahogany, but on her forehead, directly between her eyes, was a tiny white fleck, hardly even large enough to be called a star. It was the only white on the whole of her body. She was a beauty. Why would someone not want her?

"This is Roxie" said Jess, suddenly appearing from one of the sheds, carrying a rope which she handed to her father, "She's still scared stiff."

"She's a beauty" I sighed, again wishing I could own such a stunning animal. At once my mind went off on a tangent where I was very gently and carefully winning the trust of a lovely animal such as this one. I stopped dreaming with a start when something or someone nudged my arm, knocking me off balance so that I had to grab the wall. I turned sharply to see the big chestnut horse, who was now sniffing my pockets. Whatever had happened to him, he had clearly learned that humans meant food and he knew where to look as well. Hunger may have been the driving force though, I thought glumly. I now ran my eyes over this much larger horse. He was still a little on the thin side but how he had come on! His eyes were so much happier, and he was so much more relaxed than before. His coat, formerly dull and dusty was now shiny, the colour of burnished gold, or an autumn sunset. His mane and tail looked like they had never been cut, his tail almost touching the ground, a full fiery mane and tail the colour of flame... Firecrest, Wildfire, Blaze….Barney!

"Barney's really come on, hasn't he?" Jess was sitting on the gate now, swinging her feet, "Can't get over how huge he is!"

"He's so much happier" I sighed, and now I went up and patted the big horse. Barney thrust his nose into my neck and licked my ear. He clearly liked the attention and knew how to get more. I giggled as his long, overgrown mane tickled my nose and he pawed the ground with a huge hoof, pushing and nudging at me.

"He knows all about food, that one!" said Jess, "I'd love to be able to get Roxie to even do that. No idea what's happened to her but she's, what was that word you used, Dad?"

"Traumatised" replied Roger Brookes, as he struggled just trying to attach a rope to Roxie's head collar, "She's even scared of this rope. Jess has been doing some work with her while you've been away, Helen. She's getting there but it will take some doing. I don't even want to start thinking what's happened to make her so terrified. You have to be so, so careful not to startle her. But she's starting to trust Jess. She's really beginning to form a bond. You can help if you wish."

"Love to" I replied, "And what about this one?" I indicated Barney who had found a few stray wisps of hay which he was now munching. Typically, he already had a few pieces stuck in his unruly mane.

"A bit loopy for sure but there's not a bad bone in his body. He's just got out of hand because someone took him on and had no idea what they were doing. Probably scared of him, not a good way to be. Problem is the size of him and he's strong too. Bundles of energy – he could run and run. He's a young horse, I'd say a 6-year-old and he'll have a good future with the right owner."

*The right owner.* A Phrase which always made me feel a little sad. All these horses, whether I loved them or was indifferent to them, would inevitably go to someone else. Someone else would go to their stable every morning to feed them, let them out into the field, ride them, groom them, make a fuss of them. I loved taking care of all the horses but just wanted one to call my very own so that I could give him or her the care they deserved, having had such neglectful lives beforehand. I knew more than most people that caring for horses was not the glamorous lifestyle which some imagined. It was hard, physical work not to mention dirty and tiring, but worth it to spend time with these amazing animals. Some would call me soft or even crazy, but I just didn't like the idea of an animal being mistreated or neglected. I had always wanted to do my best to make sure each one was as well cared for as possible. It was never too late to give them love and care in a safe, clean environment.

"Tell you what, Helen!" grinned Jess, as she jumped off the fence and gave Barney's neck a rub as she walked by, "I'll ride Roxie, you ride Barney, and I'll see you in hospital!" I did laugh but at the moment that was how it was. Neither of these seemed ready for us to jump aboard, and when they were, I had trouble seeing it being myself or Jess. Both horses required, for the moment anyway, specialist handling. Even if we could not ride them, however, we could at least help with other aspects of their rehabilitation, a great deal of which was simply handling and TLC. Roger Brookes had a few contacts who could help out with riding if necessary. Any prospective owners would try them out before buying anyway. I went to see Heidi after that and as usual she was happy to see me, nuzzling my hair as she so often did. As I spent time making a fuss of her, I just looked at her and tried not to worry about how long she was going to be in my life.

However, I didn't have much time to think about that as Jess asked me a few minutes later,

"Oh Helen, would you like to come to the Greenwood Show next Saturday? Forecast's good and we're taking a picnic as well."

"Yes, should be good" I said, grinning to myself as I knew that Jess usually had some other reasons for going to shows other than just looking at good jumping skills and techniques.

"That new rider who's doing so well is going to be there from what people are saying. You know the one that rides Marmaduke Jinx? Super young horse, ex racehorse they say, and he's one of the brightest young riders around…."

"Oh yes, I think his name's Ian something...McNulty, McNair ? He seems to be doing very well. I've heard he's quite a looker too!" I grinned.

"Hey Helen, what are you thinking, grinning away there like the Cheshire Cat?"

"Oh nothing, just that's probably the reason you're going!" Jess blushed as she grabbed one of the plastic combs from the shelf and threw it at me.

"I don't fancy him if that's what you mean!"

"So that's why you're red in the face, then?" I teased.

"Oh get away Helen!" the two of us rushed off giggling and shoving each other around. It took my mind off Heidi for just a while...

## CHAPTER FOUR

"Are you still really sure you want to work with horses, Helen?" My mother asked me as we waited to cross a busy street in Glasgow City Centre, "There's still time to change your mind, you know."

"Look, I know you're all against me" I said, clutching the handles of all the bags to me as we waited at the lights, "But you can see how much I love them, it isn't just a passing fad. I know it isn't glamorous, in fact far from it a lot of the time. I'm sorry, Mum, but I just get sick and tired of people telling me I'm young and I'll grow out of it, like it's a pop group or something! I'm not a baby any more!"

"But , you know, if you want to think more about the subjects you're taking or anything, or you need advice, it's OK. We want the best for you Helen, and we're not going to argue with you about your choices but we've been there and we know how hard it can be, you're at a crossroads in your life…." I listened to Mum talking about the crossroads of life and wished that we could escape this particular crossroads where the traffic lights seemed to be taking forever to change. Just as I thought the traffic was slowing down, a huge, dirty truck came speeding through just as the lights changed, catching the edge of a puddle and spraying me with wet mud.

I leapt back, pushing my soggy, dirty hair out of my eyes, and glanced anxiously at the bags. They contained all my new school clothes which we had been buying and it was just typical that I should get sprayed with mud when I was ferrying these clothes home in their pristine state…

“Oh don’t worry, dear” Mum was looking sympathetically at my distraught face, “I don’t think there’s much damage and it can wash off. You can get a nice hot bath and then head out to see the horses again.” Mum was used to this by now. I seemed to end up covered from head to toe in mud or soaking wet, even when it was not my fault. So many times I had turned up at school late, wet, muddy or all three, to hear the tut-tutting in the background from people who thought they were so much better than me. I was getting used to it now! Not that I really cared what they thought any more. This was a lesson I had learned a long time ago. I was happy being Helen, and if I was not angelic or ladylike, so be it!

I couldn’t wait to get to the stables, but when I did get there, I had a strange feeling that something was not as it should be. I was very sensitive and could pick up the feelings of others like radar. Jess and her father were exchanging glances. Even Lizzie seemed a little despondent, settling down with a chew toy between her front paws, but looking up at me a little sadly, I felt.

“Great show” I said to Jess, trying to hide my anxiety as my heart began to pound, “Thanks for inviting me, I really enjoyed it.”

“Yes” said Jess rather quietly, “It was.” The show had been a fun experience for us, so there was no reason for her to be subdued.

“Look, is something wrong?” I ventured, as cold, uneasy tremor prickled my skin, making me shiver.

Jess sighed and leaned back against the door of the feed room. Deep down I knew but I really did not know how to face it.

“We’ve been trying to figure out a way to tell you” said Roger Brookes, “But you’re smart so you may well have worked this out anyway.

“It’s Heidi, isn’t it?” I sighed heavily, feeling hot tears pricking the backs of my eyes, biting my lip to fight them back, my heart suddenly heavy as stone. There was a long, ominous silence to follow, “How long?”

“She’s going two days from now” said Jess quietly.

“Two days? But how could it all be done and dusted in 2 days?”

“It wasn’t, Helen, it’s been a while. The girl’s been interested since the time that you were away and she’s tried Heidi out a few times. She had to come a few times with her parents and make sure Heidi was the right horse for her. We only arranged the payment details yesterday. She’s going to Surrey. They’re really nice people, they’re.....” But I wasn’t listening. I didn’t want to hear any more. I didn’t care how nice these people were or how rich, or how right this girl was for Heidi. It hurt me so much, hurt me that Heidi had found her forever home where she would be loved and cared for and that her forever home would not be with me. I would never see her again, never feel her warm breath on my cheek, never bury my face in her long, black mane. Cut off, just like that. Forever. I was silent for a while, trying to take this news in while my stomach churned and my head felt stretched, as if it belonged elsewhere. A feeling of unreality came over me for a minute and I had to steady myself to get my bearings.

"I'm so sorry, Helen..." Jess looked at me hopelessly, as if begging for my forgiveness.

" But not sorry enough!" I snapped, "We've been friends since we were in nursery school bur you didn't *tell* me! You kept it from me and were just going to sell her under my nose and tell me after she was gone. Is that it?"

"No Helen, you've got it wrong!" Jess's father stepped in, doing his best to sound calm, "We knew someone was interested but people have been interested in our horses before and not gone through with it. Like someone not so long ago who was interested in Roxie but changed her mind when she found out a few things about her. The girl and her parents didn't say right away that they were definitely buying Heidi. They had things to consider…." but he too trailed off, looking despondent and helpless.

"So that's it then? Back to the drawing board for good old Helen? Poor old Helen who has no money and just has to smile and be happy every time the horses she's cared for go off with someone else, never to be seen again? But oh yes, Helen's fine, Helen can cope with that, she has to make the best because she's poor and should be grateful as always!" Jess and her father were both silent now. They could have told me how they'd warned me not to get too attached to Heidi and that I should have known better but I was happy that they did not…

"Come on Helen, it's a lovely day" my mother's voice called up the stairs, "You've been in there for two whole days moping. It won't do you any good. I think you should be out enjoying the good weather. Before you know it the holidays will be over and you'll be back at school." I groaned, still feeling terrible. I had no desire to enjoy the weather even if someone had promised me it would never rain again. Life as I knew it was over now. I had written it in my diary and had not spoken to anyone since I had returned from the stables. I hadn't eaten much either, and my sleep was all over the place. I suspected that my parents had phoned Jess's house and knew the reason, as, since the night itself, they hadn't asked me what was wrong. Even Richard was keeping a low profile. He'd brought his friend Andy home the other night but apart from looking into my room and saying hello, they too had avoided me and had gone out somewhere later on.

My problem was that I was so absorbed, engrossed, even infatuated with horses and life at the stables that nothing else seemed to matter outside of that. Part of me knew it was not a good way to be, this all or nothing approach to life. It made it even more of a roller-coaster but what could I do? There were only 2 weeks left of the summer holidays now and it had not gone to plan, first with the stress and worry and having to spend time at my aunt's home, and now this. My young life was in turmoil with all the changes. I couldn't handle this. I knew that adults always talked about moving on and doing things to take your mind off whatever was bothering you, but how? Nothing mattered but the horses. But if I went now, all that would happen was that I would be given Buster or Minx to ride. I loved them dearly but both were becoming stiffer in their old age and not so capable as Heidi and I would notice the difference. However, as I have mentioned, I was a born optimist. Maybe, I pondered, I should go over there, swallow my pride and ride Minx or Buster and make up with Jess. Not that we had fallen out exactly, but after my outburst I had stormed out of the place without looking back. As was the case with Beauty before that, I avoided the stables until Heidi was gone. I didn't want to see her again, to say goodbye to her as it was far too painful. I had to start getting over her right away and seeing her again would not help at all. It also gave me some time and space to clear my mind before going back to One Tree Farm again.

Fear and trepidation took over me as I rode my old bicycle up to Jess's place and laid it up against the wall. However, I needn't have worried, as I was first greeted by Lizzie the Beagle, then Jess herself. I saw Jess's sister Meghan in the background as well, looking curiously on, but she quickly called Lizzie in and disappeared.

To my surprise, Jess came rushing up and hugged me.

"Helen!" she was almost in tears now, "I knew you'd come back! I know it was awful for you and we felt so helpless because you and Heidi were made for each other." But despite this, I knew Heidi was already long gone and, more importantly, she was eternally lost to me. The world would not stop turning because my favourite horse was gone for good, nor did I expect it to. I knew I would get back to normal and accept the inevitable but it was always so hard to be in this place, feeling so lost, and not even knowing where to start. Yet I was also angry with myself for falling for Heidi after what had happened with Beauty. What was wrong with me? Why couldn't I just switch off feelings or not show them, like the adults seemed to do?

I just hoped that Jess and her family had not been setting the world to rights, trying to think of a cheering up Helen campaign as I didn't need that. I needed to do something else, to move on.

"Do you want to help us in the yard?" Jess asked, "Dad's been working with both Roxie and Barney and said we can help. Oh and he said we can have crash helmets, parachutes and shin pads if we need them!" I had to smile at that, and with some difficulty, I pushed the disappointment of losing Heidi to one side and followed her.

Both horses were tied up in the yard. The grooming kits were out and Roger Brookes greeted us with a grin.

"Right girls, all hands to the grindstone" he said, "These two need grooming because they've been out in the field rolling about. Roxie especially needs the contact so if you could give them both the once over." I thought Jess would shy from Roxie who was already rolling her eyes and backing anxiously away but, obviously having done a lot of work with the mare since her arrival, Jess took the grooming kit and went quietly up to her, talking to her and approaching with caution. I turned my attention to Barney.

Again, the big chestnut horse nudged me expectantly, seeking whatever treats I had in my pocket and luckily I had some carrot sticks still remaining. They had been there a few days and were slightly the worse for wear but he didn't seem to mind as he munched happily. As before, he butted me and almost sent me flying, such was his size and power. I had started to realise something about this horse. He was big and had seemed so imposing at first but there was no malice in him at all. He did not appear unduly nervous and was happy to stand quietly as I started the task of tidying him up. It was not easy at my size but luckily there were step ladders and boxes to stand on, helping me reach the highest point of Barney's back which was very dusty and covered in dried mud. Maybe, I thought, I should transfer my affections to this big horse now that Heidi was beyond my reach. It was not so easy, however. My bond with Heidi had developed over time. She was a horse of the right size and temperament for me. This was not. Not only was Barney a large adult's horse by most people's standards, but from what was said, he was unpredictable to ride and needed training, presumably by someone who had some weight behind them in order to steady the ship if things got out of control. But then again, with a horse I had no possibility of forming a horse/rider relationship with, maybe I would be less attached and more able to let Barney go when the time inevitably came.

Jess's father had one more surprise in store. Jess obviously knew about it as she smiled quietly to herself as she finished grooming Roxie as best she could, and I noted that she was doing well in keeping the mare calm.

"Right, I hope you girls are up for this" he said. I glanced up to see Roger Brookes carrying a lunge rein, "I just need to lunge these two but with a little bit of weight on their backs."

"You mean we're going to *ride* them?" I was aghast.

"Yes. We haven't tried anything like that with either but I figured if we try them out with someone light on board to start off, it'll be easier for them to adjust. They've both been ridden before, just probably not recently and not very well. We don't know, they might have had badly fitting saddles or bridles and that can cause lots of problems and really upset them." Before I had time to even think about it, I was hoisted bareback onto the massive horse. I felt a slight panic going through me as I took in the massive bulk of the neck and the fact there was so much horse in front of me and behind me. The copper-coloured mane seemed to go on forever and when the big horse shook his head, I nearly lost my grip. I was apparently going first. I was used to riding bareback but not on a totally strange, massive and unpredictable young horse like Barney.

The advantage of lunging is that the person in the middle of the circle has control of the horse (or should have) enabling the rider to concentrate on what they are doing and less on the control of the horse. If I was surprised at Roger Brookes taking this step, I hadn't much time to think about it. If he asked me to work with a horse, I considered that he thought I was up to it. I guessed that he and Jess had discussed me but I was not annoyed, quite the opposite in fact. If this was a tactic to take my mind off the loss of Heidi, it was certainly a good one.

As Roger Brookes from the ground gave Barney the command to trot, I made a sudden realisation. I was really enjoying this! Barney was a big and powerful horse and his stride covered the ground at an amazing rate, so smooth and steady. He was definitely the biggest horse I had ever ridden and I began to feel my happiness slowly ebb back. I knew I could never have the bond I'd had with Heidi ever again, and I would never let myself become so attached to a horse ever again, knowing that a mere sum of money could take him or her away literally overnight, never to be seen again. But today I had reached a milestone. I realised that I had covered new ground. I had been on board one of the more difficult new horses and was actually enjoying it. Now that this step had been taken, I knew I was ready to work with Barney, another horse I had no chance of owning. But now I knew that. I had been warned, I was the one to blame for getting upset over Heidi. It was a mistake that I promised myself there and then I would never make again.

## CHAPTER FIVE

"It must be so good to be free of school and have a job" I sighed, as I watched Richard's friend Andy working on a car at the local garage, "Having your own money to spend and not having your parents telling you what to do all the time!"

"I'm sorry to say" Andy slid out from under the bonnet again, grinning at me, "The working life isn't all it's cracked up to be. Often you end up doing the same thing day in, day out, and I still have to live with my parents and they keep telling me to tidy my room! If I'm in late I've to make my own food too! It's only the very rich working folk that can do what they want I suppose!"

"They all tell me I won't earn much working with horses."

"Well, you won't, simple as that. I don't earn a lot working with cars, not at the moment anyway, but I could maybe get a better job in the future, you know, chauffeur or some rich lord or lady somewhere! Some people think working with cars is glamorous but as you can see, it's not. I don't think working with horses would be all that glamorous either."

"Far from it!" I sighed, "Covered in filth from top to toe, long hours and not much money. A lot of folks who work with horses have no social lives and end up staying single, not that I'm worried about that."

"No school teacher proposed marriage yet, then?" Andy grinned at me.

"I've already told you, I don't fancy any of my teachers!" I rolled my eyes to Heaven, as I did when people didn't seem to believe that I didn't have designs on any males! "And in case it's escaped your notice, I'm fourteen!"

"Nothing like starting young" laughed Andy, "Anyway, you might not be so badly off if you end up being a famous showjumper!"

"Riding what?" I sighed, "I don't even have a horse of my own. The way things are going I'll be lucky if I end up being Jess's groom when *she's* famous!"

"You'd do it though, if you got the chance?"

"Oh yes, I certainly would." Andy was a good friend and I loved to chat to him. He had a good sense of humour and I didn't need to worry about my appearance when he was usually clad in greasy overalls, with oil and dirt smeared across his suntanned face as he scrambled around under a client's car.

At the stables things were actually going well. I had noticed the great improvement in Roxie with Jess's handling of her. Gaining the trust of such a traumatised animal could be a long process but Jess was already showing so much patience and I was really impressed. She was also making sure to ride and pay attention to her own horse, Mary Rose. A few times she let me ride Mary Rose while she rode Buster, which was really lovely of her.

Jess's father Roger was still lunging us both regularly. One day I asked Jess why she always rode Roxie and I rode Barney.

"You're joking, Helen!" was her reply, "Me ride that? Dad asked me first if I wanted to ride him and then told me a few things about him that put me off! So he's all yours!"

"What things, Jess?"

"Oh I wouldn't worry" said Jess, "But you do have to wonder why he's ended up here, a fit young horse like that. Not sure how he would be if you rode him off the lunge." I shuddered when I thought of how big and strong Barney was and what he would be like out of control, galloping at full tilt...it may really be best not to know. I liked the big chestnut horse and found him very friendly and easy to handle, but at the same time I wished a more suitable mount would arrive at the yard. At the moment, Roxie didn't look to be that horse either, especially with Jess seemingly so attached to her. It was a dilemma for me though. Should another more suitable horse appear on the scene, I could end up very attached to him or her and that would be problematic again. Another Heidi scenario could be another negative experience for me! I was angry with myself for becoming so hopelessly attached, but hard as I tried, it seemed to keep happening, as it had with Beauty before that. Also, although I did not want to admit it, every time it happened it was just that little bit harder, that little bit more painful for me. It was as if I was scarred a little deeper, a little more permanently each time.

We walked down to the stables and were surprised to find that both Roxie and Barney were ready to be ridden, complete with their saddles and bridles and looking very smart and businesslike.

"Please tell me this is just a trial to make sure their tack fits them!" said Jess to her father as he appeared with a big grin on his face. Roger Brookes grinned at his daughter but neither denied or confirmed if that was the case.

"Time to move on and see how they go in the field" he said. As he passed Roxie she backed away and almost collided with the wall, giving herself a huge fright and almost breaking through the fence. Barney meantime was sifting through bits and pieces on the ground, still looking for any snippets of hay he may have missed out on. His jaws seemed to be going continuously, but this was a sign that he was calm and settled, unlike Roxie who tended to stand with her head held high, her eyes showing white as if she expected danger to jump out at her from every possible direction.

I was beyond feeling unwell now as so many things had been sprung on us. Just then we heard a joyful bark and Lizzie the Beagle rushed up, accompanied by Jess's sister Meghan. She had no real interest in horses but she glanced over this unlikely pair and said,

"Are you two going to ride them?" Jess nodded solemnly.

"You're crazy!" observed Meghan, "Rather you than me!" then she called Lizzie to heel and continued with her walk over the fields.

Without further ado, Roger Brookes helped us both aboard our respective mounts. I tried not to shake with fear as the ground disappeared into the distance. Under me, the whole animal just felt like a mountain but it was a live mountain, a volcano the colour of fire, ready to go and ready to bolt with me or do anything at all that he fancied. With Jess and I both mounted, Roger carefully unhooked the field gate and swung it gently open. Even the sight of the gate had Roxie shying away and it was all Jess could do to stay aboard. It was not an auspicious start to say the least.

The first few steps of the walk in the field went well, but that was short-lived. Still not recovered from her fright with the gate, Roxie was on edge, walking with her head and tail held high, her eyes still showing flecks of white as she stared suspiciously around her. Then suddenly, it happened. Obviously startled by the noise and our sudden appearance, a rabbit darted out at the speed of light, from right under Roxie's nose. That was by far the last straw. Roxie launched herself into the air and promptly took off up the hill at top speed, a terrified looking Jess hanging on for grim death. I was alert but not alert enough for that. I made a frantic grab at Barney's reins in a vain attempt to reel him in, but it was too late. Seeing Roxie careering off into the distance, he clearly thought this was a free for all. He plunged like one of those rodeo horses on TV, reminding me of a big dipper I'd been on last summer, and took off. As he did so, he stuck his head between his knees and leapt into the air, his back legs kicking out behind him like those of a kangaroo. His entire back arched strongly, giving me very little chance of hanging on. I clutched the reins and a handful of rust-coloured mane desperately and decided to go with the flow. Being a young horse, Barney clearly felt that this was a bit of fun and was really enjoying it. He galloped flat out for a bit, fairly covering the ground as he tried to catch up with Roxie, already at the top of the hill clattering around among the trees with Jess still clamped over her back like a limpet, just trying to hang on the same as me.

Just when I thought I was winning the battle and managing to get my massive mount under control, Barney decided to do one last rodeo style stunt. His head disappeared between his knees and his powerful backbone arched into a spectacular buck, flinging me forward onto his neck. I scrabbled frantically for control but this was just one too many for me. The force of gravity was against me as I tipped forward, staring at the horse's shoulders upside down before I plunged forward, flying through the air and hitting the ground with an almighty thump which knocked all the breath out of me and left me stunned for quite a few seconds.

"Helen! Helen! Are you OK?" vaguely, above me, I heard Jess's father's voice sounding out of breath as he had obviously rushed to our aid. It took me a few moments to get my own breath back and I realised I was staring up into the very muddy and shocked looking face of my best friend, also breathless and shaken.

“I’ll live” I sighed, struggling shakily to my feet and dusting myself down.

“Went well, I thought!” said Jess and the three of us burst into laughter. We could see the two horses grazing a little distance away looking none the worse. It was the sort of thing that happened fairly regularly with horses - the unpredictable nature of the sport was probably what made it all the more exciting. This was why some people thought us totally crazy for even getting onto a horse’s back in the first place, especially when they were as unpredictable as Barney and Roxie. Both of them had surpassed themselves today!

As I went to bed that night, exhausted and aching but otherwise unscathed, I found myself wishing and hoping that a horse who was suitable for me to ride, a horse like Heidi, would finally arrive at the stables. And one day, some way, my family and I may by some miracle be able to afford to buy it.

## CHAPTER SIX

It all started one evening when dinner time was drawing closer and there was no sign of my older brother Richard. As I was a fast runner, my parents dispatched me to the garage to try and hurry him along.

I saw no one as I approached the workshop door and my heart sank. I looked round, wondering if Andy happened to be around, and if so he may know Richard's whereabouts. However, I was completely surprised when a totally strange young man appeared from behind a car and said with a smile,

"Can I help you at all?"

"I hope so?" I replied, "I'm looking for Richard. Have you see him ?"

"Sure, he went out about half an hour ago to get some bits and pieces. He said he'd just go straight home after he gets them because we won't need them until tomorrow. I take it you're his sister, aren't you?"

"Yes, my name's Helen."

"Derek" he said, stretching his hand out to me, while I frantically examined mine to ensure they were fit for the purpose of shaking without leaving Derek with something highly unpleasant to remember me by...it had happened before after all!

He had a firm, warm handshake and as we shook hands, he looked right at me. He had longish dark brown hair and big, friendly dark eyes. I liked him instantly.

"You don't know me" he continued, "I'm new here, I'm doing an apprenticeship. I take it you're still at school."

"Yes, for my sins. Quite a few people I know are older and working and I can't wait to get to that stage."

"Be careful what you wish for" said Derek, "My mum and dad are still giving me grief about my messy room and now it's all the oily overalls in their washing machine they're moaning about. Whatever stage you're at in life, they seem to be having a go! You'd think they'd be glad about me earning a wage and all, but seemingly not!"

"Well, I'll take your word for it!" I laughed.

I went to the stables later on and was surprised to see a horsebox being unloaded. A neat looking grey horse was being led carefully out by Roger Brookes and it was clear that he was limping quite badly. Jess was there already, watching with interest. All the other horses were out in the field, including Roxie and Barney who were now quite well settled at One Tree Farm.

"This is Dylan" said Jess, "Rider couldn't control him and had an accident, fell into a hedge or something, that's how the story goes anyway. The horse gets the blame of course and they get rid of him!"

"So is this your new ride, Jess?" I gave her a little nudge.

"Not really" she said, "I'd sooner ride Barney!" and we both giggled.

However, there was not a great deal left of the school holidays and the school uniform, which had mercifully suffered no real damage when a truck splashed me with mud had been tried on and adjusted. I didn't really want to think about the dreaded day when we had to return to school again, one year older and with more serious studying to do. I was worried that I would lose valuable time with the horses, but at the same time, I didn't want to go too much the other way and fail my exams.

On the night before school started again, I was at the stables with Jess although naturally we had instructions not to stay out too late as we had such a big day ahead. We sat on the yard gate swinging our feet, and watched the horses grazing in the field. It was such a peaceful scene, looking at their silhouettes in the lengthening shadows as the sun began to set.

"Seen that new guy at the garage?" Jess asked, swinging her feet.

"You mean Derek?"

"Derek is it? Wow, you're off to a flying start!"

“I don’t fancy him or anything! I just happened to bump into him because he was there when I was looking for Richard. You know what his time keeping’s like!”

“Richard’s never been in time for anything in his life!” said Jess with a grin, “Derek’s quite good looking though. How old do you reckon? Seventeen? Eighteen?”

“Maybe” I sighed, my interest already on the wane. I studied the shapes of the horses as they gradually drifted over to the band of trees on the hill where they became less visible. All of them were out there except for Dylan who was being kept in a stable to have his injuries treated and monitored. I was already miles away, imagining myself soaring over high jumps on a perfect horse, forgetting for a moment that it was not a good idea to fall in love with any of the horses Roger Brookes acquired. I was allowed to dream just for a moment or two, though. Let them dream about boys; I dreamed about horses.

“Helen! You’re miles away!” Jess was looking right at me, an amused expression on her face, “Got some dreamy guy lined up somewhere?”

“You know me, Jess, too busy dreaming about horses!”

“Think big, girl!” Jess patted me on the shoulder, “Dreams don’t cost anything. You never know what's going to happen in life so we're best just to go with the flow."

"Exactly! And that's why I don't want to be tying myself down to any guys and worse still, having babies! I'm not even fifteen and I plan to enjoy it while I can! I don't really fancy being old."

"False teeth and polyester frocks?" Jess and I both giggled.

"Anyway, looks like we're back to doing this in the evenings and weekends only, plus the homework! So, does your dad have anything in mind?"

"Sure, he wants us to ride Roxie and Barney at a show" replied Jess. But she was joking, and I gave her a little slap.

"When I mentioned old age, I do actually want to be around a little bit longer!" I said, "Seriously though, do you think these two will ever find forever homes?"

"I'd like to hope so" sighed Jess, running a hand through her hair, "We can't keep them here forever, it wouldn't be good for them anyway. There's no harm in either of those horses but they've both got issues and they need a lot of work and very special owners." Much as I liked Roxie and Barney, and enjoyed working with them, I felt guilty for secretly wishing they would move on soon, so that there would be more space to accommodate new horses which may be more suitable for us to ride. Four rescue horses at once was the absolute maximum.

The first day of school did eventually come. Despite the dreaded onslaught of hours in the classroom and mountains of homework, there was an air of cheerfulness about the place as it was after all good to meet up again with those we hadn't seen for many weeks. Some were less welcome of course. There was a new teacher this year as well, a maths teacher called Mr Gallagher who some of the girls were already swooning over. I didn't hold out much hope as I was so terrible at maths that I didn't see how even the world's most handsome man could get me through the exam!

However, I was as relieved as anyone when the bell rang to announce the end of the day, and a tidal wave of pupils swelled towards the exits. Getting onto the school bus was always fairly easy as long as you allowed yourself just to be swept along in the raging torrent of energy which seemed to erupt once the school day was done.

Today, however, when I came out of the newsagents shop clutching my well-earned bag of sweets, I walked straight into someone who was coming into the shop, almost losing my balance completely. The most important thing was to hang onto my bag of sweets of course!

"Oh sorry!" said a vaguely familiar voice, "We met the other day, didn't we? Helen, isn't it?"

"Yes!" I said, looking up quickly, "Oh hello Derek. We meet again! Sorry about that, wasn't looking where I was going!"

"Oh don't worry!" grinned Derek, who was dressed in jeans and a denim jacket which I thought really suited him, "I do things like that all the time! I'm really clumsy!"

"So am I!" I laughed, "Would you like one of my sweets?" Jess came out of the shop a little behind me as it turned out that she had met a friend inside the shop.

"Oh hello Derek!" she said, "Fancy meeting you again!"

"Well your friend here just walked right into me!" joked Derek, smiling at us both.

"Well, why don't you cash in and come and see us in action?" said Jess boldly.

"Oh yes, you have horses, don't you?"

"My dad has his ear to the ground in horsey circles and he takes in horses that have been a bit unlucky to bring them on. Helen and I give him a hand when we can. Some of the horses are really crazy though."

"Sounds like fun!" said Derek, "I don't ride at all but I wouldn't mind watching you two in action."

An hour or so later, Derek sat on the gate watching our efforts with Roxie and Barney. Dylan was still off limits as he would not be fit enough for quite a while. This evening, Roger Brookes was just getting the two horses to accept a lot of handling and people around them, putting things on their backs and taking them off again. This exercise seemed a lot easier for Barney than it was for Roxie. The mare was head shy, not trusting anyone who came too close to touching her head. It made me wonder what she had endured in her short life. I tried not to think too much, as cruelty to animals was something I hardly dared to consider at any length. It literally turned my stomach. I was unsure if Barney had been cruelly treated or just neglected. I suspected his former owner would have been scared of his size and power, just simply not an experienced or sympathetic enough rider to see the project through. Neither of these fine animals had really been given a chance. They were simply victims of circumstance.

They both looked so much better now that they had gained weight and had some shine on their coats. Roxie's dark coffee-coloured coat sparkled in the sun while Barney's glowed like fire. I remembered the days before I even knew his name, and had imagined him to be called Flame, Wildfire, Firestorm or something along those lines. I was almost disappointed at first that he was called Barney, but not now. In fact it suited him and it was an ideal name. The horses kept the original names they had been given and they were not usually changed. Some of them would be named by their previous owners or may just have been given a name to identify them while they were transitory. Barney's mane and tail were long and flowing, and when the sun caught him, he really looked as if he were on fire, glowing and warm like an autumn sunset.

Now that he was approaching the peak of his weight and condition, the powerful neck and shoulder muscles were clearer and more defined than before, as they rippled under the flame-red coat.

While I was busy tidying up afterwards, I realised that Jess seemed to be getting on very well with Derek.

"Are you interested in learning to ride?" I heard her say, "Because we've got Buster and Minx, pretty much pets - they're getting on and we don't ride them a lot but they're really quiet. It doesn't matter what you wear, just something sensible…." I chuckled to myself as they drifted out of earshot. Even Jess's head was being turned by boys now, but not mine. Derek was attractive but not for me. I was dedicated to my cause and intended to stay that way. And when I was determined to do something I was really determined...

## CHAPTER SEVEN

Although I was very single-minded and dedicated to my heart's desire of being with horses and working with horses, I knew I had to have my feet firmly on the ground too. I was not a naturally studious person. I was far more likely to spend my class time gazing out of the window at the skyline, imagining I was out riding over the fields with Jess. I just stopped occasionally to check my watch to see how much longer I had to endure my class!

However I did acknowledge, albeit reluctantly, that what my parents said was correct. By failing my exams and leaving school early, I would significantly reduce my career options. I was still only fourteen and it was very hard to imagine myself working in any job but I had to try. Although I had heard Richard talking about a few of his friends who failed exams and managed to resit and pass them at college later, it sounded rather difficult as they were mostly working as well. Besides, I did not like the idea of sitting exams at all and did not want to have the dubious "pleasure" of enduring them more than once!

It was a dilemma but one I would have to deal with. I could not let the horses distract me from my studies too much, but in turn the studies were not going to get in the way of my dreams about horses. My plate was getting fuller but I just had to keep my feet on the ground. I was primarily a very practical person and my head was not easily turned.

I decided, reluctantly, to miss a week at the stables and really work hard at the maths, my worst subject. I got some extra French in as well. I spoke to Jess on the phone and she told me that someone was interested in Roxie. I was quite surprised.

"This lady's really fallen for her" Jess said, "She's even ridden her, she got aboard much more bravely than I ever did. She just seemed to know how to ride her, they suit each other. She's made no offer yet but Dad's hopeful. I must say I'm surprised. Are you?"

"Yes" I said, "She's a lovely horse actually, but just so scared of everything. I thought it would take longer to move her on, really I did. Are you sad, Jess? I know you like her."

"I do like her, she's lovely" said Jess, "But it's the way it has to be, the more you fall in love the harder it is when they do go. I'm just trying to be positive because she looks like finding her ideal forever home. It's what all these horses really deserve above all else."

"Never mind Jess, you can still ride Barney!" I teased her.

"Oh, and Barney's still with us" said Jess, "Nearly knocked me flying yesterday because I gave him an apple and he head butted me right in the ribs! Dad said that was him showing his appreciation! You're welcome to him, Helen, you really are!"

"And how's Dylan?"

"Doing great. The vet says he should be ready for some light exercise in a few more weeks. You never know, that could be my next big ride!"

"How do you know he isn't another bucking bronco, Jess?" I laughed.

"I'll just have to wait and hope! Anyway, enjoy the homework!" I sighed heavily as I put the phone down. I was trying, really I was, but maths simply was not my subject.

When I finally did return to the stables, I was in for a surprise. It was not the fact that Lizzie the Beagle was rushing around my feet with a grooming brush in her mouth, but the fact that the new garage apprentice, Derek, was being led round the field on board Buster, and Jess was the one doing the leading. I wondered again if Jess was falling under his spell and chuckled to myself. However, there was an uneasy feeling in the back of my mind. Something I couldn't quite describe. As I could not interpret the feeling, whatever it was, I pushed it out of my mind rather than try and unravel and deal with it now.

When they saw me standing by the fence, Jess led Buster over so that we could all have a chat.

"You're a quick mover, Jess!" I laughed, and Derek, who looked relaxed aboard the horse, grinned at me too.

"Jess and I are just mates, Helen!" he remarked, giving me what I thought was rather a strange look. He appeared to exchange a very quick glance with Jess too, and I wondered if there was a conspiracy afoot!

"No comment, but I do wonder why you felt the need to spell that out, Derek?"

"No reason, just don't want the wedding invitations going out just yet, that's all!"

"I'm fourteen, Derek!" said Jess, and we all laughed. Jess continued to lead Derek around and I joined them. She was basically just showing him the basics of riding a horse at the moment, so nothing too strenuous. As we walked round, we heard whinnying and Barney, Roxie, Minx and Mary Rose came rushing up to the fence to stare over at us, in the hope of something nice to eat. Derek laughed,

"I've just been thinking, Helen, that's some size of a horse, that ginger one, you're so brave to even think about getting on him."

"Barney's actually not so bad once you get to know him. He's just like a kid who hasn't been allowed out to use up his energy. Not a bad bone in his body. He's just very strong!" I was being subtle or else I would no doubt have pointed out that horses are not described as "ginger", as the word is "chestnut!" I glanced at the 4 eager heads looking over the fence and felt warm inside, knowing that these were horses who were safe in a world where so many animals were abandoned, neglected and badly treated. We could not save every one in the world but we could help just one little selection to live out their ideal lives.

Even once the riding lesson was over and Buster had been turned out to join the others in the field, Derek did not seem keen to leave. It was a little strange, especially since he had been at pains to point out that any relationship between himself and Jess was purely platonic. I glanced sideways at Derek, hoping to catch him at a moment when he was not aware of my gaze on him. Despite myself, I did admire his dark eyelashes and the sweep of his longish, dark hair. I simply didn't understand what I was feeling. I had wondered earlier, as it was as if I had an anger or scorn towards Jess for being so taken with Derek, as if the two of them were pairing up and leaving me out as the baggage, the unwanted gooseberry. I almost stopped dead in my tracks. I was jealous. But why? Derek was kind, funny, gentle, mature, dark and good looking...but no, I didn't fancy him at all, of course I didn't! I was Helen Doyle, single-minded to the death, and a mere boy wasn't going to turn my head, was he? Derek was not a boy of my own age though, he was a young man, already working and making a life for himself.

As I tried to sort out the mess of confusing feelings in my head, I realised, to my horror, that I had been staring at Derek while I was miles away in thought, and he was now looking at me. Fortunately he did not look angry, more bemused than anything else.

“Are you OK, Helen?” he asked at length, “You look like you’ve seen a ghost!”

"Oh sorry, I didn't mean to stare at you! I was just thinking and I was miles away. It's all this extra homework and studying I've had to catch up on. Oh, I must sound like such a bore!"

"You're not a bore!" Derek looked at me in a way I had never been looked at before, his gaze lingering on me as if he was thinking or trying to work something out, "But it does sound like you work too hard! I know the feeling though, I took physics and I really had to work hard at it, my parents were always breathing down my neck and they really wanted me to go to Uni but I just wanted to work with cars!" We were now at the far end of the stable yard, near the back door of the Brookes' home. I wondered where Jess was. I felt she may be tidying up for the evening and that I should be helping her.

"Well believe it or not, it's the same for me. I want to work with horses. You guessed?" he nodded and grinned, "I just want to work in a yard a bit like this one but my folks say I should keep my options open and failing my exams is *not* one of those options. I know they're right but it's hard just to sit down and get the work done."

"Well, why not have a break? A few of us could go out, just to the cinema or to a cafe or for a meal, just maybe 4 or 5 of us. I can't see your mum and dad objecting to that."

I felt like asking him why he was talking to me like this, why he seemed to be trying to befriend me. I even wondered if he felt slightly sorry for me and was trying to include me now, because he could see that I felt a bit jealous of his attention to Jess. But surely if he and Jess were an item, or it was going that way, he would want to be alone with her? It could simply be that he was making a friendly gesture to get a few of us together to take our minds off work and study.

"That sounds like a good idea" I said, not really holding out much hope that it would actually go ahead, "I think we should be helping Jess tidy up for the night, unless you have to rush off."

"No" said Derek, "Just show me what needs doing and I'll help you do it."

The very next day I woke up in a sweat, hardly believing what I had dreamed. I had been walking down the street hand in hand with Derek, and when we reached the end of the street he turned and kissed me. That was when I woke up. I was astounded at myself. What had possessed me to dream that? I wasn't responsible for the content of my dreams, or was I? My mother had studied psychology and often spoke of Sigmund Freud who noted what people dreamed and psychoanalysed them. What would he have made of me? That I was a desperate sex fiend, or just a tearaway, too lazy to do my studying?

However, I had come to a conclusion. I had been in denial about something for quite a while now. I had tried to cover it up, run away from it and change the subject but the fact remained. For the first time in my life, my head had been seriously turned by a member of the opposite sex...I had a massive crush on Derek!

I really had to keep this to myself. If Jess thought I was acting oddly, she did not comment on it. I did not mention Derek and tried to show no emotion if his name came up. I concentrated on my school work as much as I possibly could. On the homeward bound school bus one Wednesday afternoon, we ended up sitting behind Samantha Inglis who was bragging to her friend Charlotte about how clever her boyfriend was and that when the time came, he was bound to be accepted for Oxford or Cambridge. Once again I thought that, for someone with such a perfect life including the picture perfect boyfriend, Samantha spent rather a lot of her time picking holes in other people's lives and relationships! Seeing us, she turned round and I groaned silently.

"I've heard you're seeing a guy, Jess, a mechanic! A bit beneath you, surely?"

"Maybe you should be careful what gossip you listen to, Samantha!" said Jess flatly. She was clearly trying not to rise to the bait, but Samantha was persistent.

"I mean I could understand if it was Helen. Her mum and dad can't afford anything so it makes sense that she'd plump for a mechanic. After all, she's always had a soft spot for *him* whatever his name is!" she indicated Terry who was driving along whistling as he so often did.

"*He* has a name and Terry and I are just mates for goodness sake!" it was my turn to get cross. I had no romantic feelings for anyone, at least I tried to convince myself that was the case for now, but what I did object to was someone putting down my friends. Unlike Samantha, I did not judge people by their job, their upbringing or how much money they or their parents did or did not have.

Samantha, however, was unrelenting, "So it's Terry now, is it? My Dad says bus drivers are common and the little they do earn goes on drink and the bookies. And besides, he's miles older than you. Don't you know that's an offence?"

"No I didn't know it was an offence to be friendly with someone, Samantha. But it should be an offence to have to listen to the likes of you!"

"So what do you think of Jess going with Metal Mickey, the grease monkey then? Are you jealous? Oh no, of course you're in love with horses, aren't you? You're just plain weird, you know!" I was so, so tempted, to slap her really hard across the face that I almost had to clamp my fingers to the bus seat. However, I was not going to rise to it. She had taunted me so often but I did still wonder about Jess and Derek. Perhaps they were an item after all, and they were trying to make it look like the opposite because of the reaction that some people may have, some of the prejudiced people who judged by wealth and status? Perhaps they needed me as an ally and this was why Derek seemed to be planning some kind of rendezvous to possibly discuss this.

Finally we reached our stop. As I rose to collect my things and get off, I glared at Samantha and she ignored me. As I reached the bus doors, Terry said,

"Never mind her, Helen. She's stuck up, but you know that." I was surprised as I hadn't realised Terry was even aware of the conversation but right enough, the volume must have been quite high. I was so angry with Samantha that I was unable to speak so I smiled at Terry and said goodbye, feeing instantly better.

However, my troubles for the day were not over. In my haste, I had not checked that my shoelaces were tied. As I stepped off the platform, smiling sweetly at Terry, I totally lost my balance and sprawled headlong on the hard pavement, which was unrelenting and jarred every bone in my body. I heard laughter in the background but the concerned tones of Terry and Jess were much closer fortunately. As I started to struggle, I realised I was wet too so there was obviously some mud – great! I then felt a strong arm on my shoulder, gently easing me to my feet. I turned slowly, just expecting it to be Terry, but to my surprise, it was Derek.

"Are you OK, Helen?" he said, sounding genuinely concerned, "That was quite a tumble!" The school bus was stationary in the background, Terry and Jess looking on, concerned but silent. I heard no more hilarity from Samantha so wondered if one or both of them had told her off.

"Don't worry, I'll look after her from here" said Derek,surprisingly, putting his arm round me as I finally was on my feet, bloodied and battered, but no serious damage done.

"If you're sure you're OK, Helen." said Terry.

"Thanks for your help, Terry" I said, giving him a watery smile, "It seems I'll be taken care of now."

# CHAPTER EIGHT

My confused and tired mind was full of questions, the main one being why Derek was there. Why was he so often there when the school bus arrived? However, I was in pain and discomfort and knew there was mud on my face and that my hair was tangled, with blood in it.  Not ideal when I had admitted to myself only recently that I had a crush on Derek.  He was clearly a kind young man but any hope I had of securing him as a romantic partner dissolved in those first few minutes after the mishap. Derek led me straight into the newsagents and, taking one look at the state of me, Gail the shop owner who knew me well, rushed to get a chair for me.

"Helen took a tumble off the bus"  explained Derek, "Nothing serious but she's shaken up."

"No problem Helen, I'll get some warm water and a few bits and pieces from the back shop."  The door opened then and Jess came in, slightly breathless.

"Sorry, couldn't get away from Terry.  He's quite worried about you, you know.  I had to virtually chase him away in the end, but I tell you he didn't half tell Samantha off, that made my day!  I didn't realise Terry cared so much!"  she grinned.

"Terry?"  Derek raised a curious eyebrow.

“The school bus driver” I said by way of explanation.

“Oh yes” said Derek, “He did seem really concerned.” he grinned at Jess then.

“Oh come on, Jess! Me and Terry? You’re kidding! We’re just mates, always have been!”

“So why are you at pains to point this out, Helen, the fact that there’s nothing between you and Terry?”

“Because I’m fourteen” I said, trying not to laugh as I repeated the conversation from the other day, “And I don’t want the wedding invitations going out just yet!”

“Go on then, admit it!” Derek teased me, as Gail brought the first aid kit out and started tending to my cuts and bruises.

“Admit what?”

“You’re a fare dodger!”

“Well that’s true! We just became friends because I’m so clumsy. Believe it or not, how to make friends and influence people….just come equipped with two left feet and fall over everything in sight. I fell down the stairs on the bus when I was about 12 and then I fell on the floor of the bus and now I’ve done it again today. We just started talking and he’s got a wacky sense of humour so we hit it off. But that’s all. I’m not going out with him but if

Samantha wants to think that, tough! She's just jealous!"

"That's the spirit!" said Derek, "Maybe she fancies him herself? But I take it we're giving the horses a miss tonight?"

"I think I'll have to" I admitted somewhat reluctantly, "I'm aching all over. The thought of Barney bouncing around makes me feel a bit sick."

"I wonder what sort of person will get Barney?"said Jess, "I mean he's a challenge. He's actually got a lovely nature but the problem is his size and strength and the fact he's full of beans. He needs someone really dedicated to working with him and spending a lot of time and effort with him. He'd be worth it though. Dad actually said he's an Irish bred horse and he's got a bit of Irish Draft in him, that's where the size and strength comes from!"

I felt a lot better once Gail had finished patching me up. Another surprise was in store. As I got up slowly and carefully to leave the shop, Gail handed me a paper bag.

"All your favourites are in here" she said, and when she saw me starting to look around for my purse, "On the house. You deserve it. Thank your friend here, it was his suggestion!" Gail eyed Derek then looked from him to me, as if trying to work out if we were dating each other, but she wisely said no more.

A few days later I was back to my usual self. It was a weekend with nice weather and no other commitments. No family visits, all homework and studying out of the way earlier in the week, so I was free to do nothing else but spend time with Jess and the horses.

Despite our earlier reservations, Jess and I were managing Barney and Roxie much better than expected. Both were very challenging and a little unpredictable but the signs were positive. We hadn't been put off by what we now referred to as the "rodeo incident" and had in fact had several more incidents since then, but nothing serious. If I had been scared by the big chestnut horse to begin with, I was far more relaxed now and could see that Jess was the same with Roxie.

Roger Brookes tended not to tell us what he planned to get us to do in advance, probably so as not to worry us. I was somewhat alarmed, however, when I saw that some small jumps had been erected in the field.

First of all he just wanted us to warm them up gently and that went well. However, he had to leave us to it for a few minutes as a strange woman appeared by the field gate and Roger Brookes went over to have a word with her.

"She's the one" said Jess at once, "The one who's interested in Roxie." I couldn't quite see her properly but hoped she would give Roxie a good home, "Hope she doesn't want to ride her right now, I'm looking forward to the jumping." I didn't say anything but I seriously was not.

Then, out of the blue, Jess surprised me by saying, "You fancy him, don't you?" I swung round in the saddle as we walked the horses round together, and found her looking right at me.

"I don't know what you mean!" I looked away quickly, but it was too late. Jess was no fool and I knew that she had sussed me out.

"Derek Hall of course. Who else would I be meaning?"

"Terry apparently!" I giggled, "Some people seem to think I've got several men on the go! Anyway, what if I did fancy Derek? I know you like him and he likes you!"

"Is that what you think?" Jess sounded genuinely surprised, "We told you, me and Derek are friends. To be honest, he's not really my type."

"Let me guess, you're still carrying a torch for Ian the showjumper?"

"Yes, actually" said Jess, and it was her turn to look away, "Not that he'd ever notice the likes of me. He's doing so well that lots of girls are after him. His horse Marmaduke is really amazing too."

"You're amazing, Jess!" I said, "And don't forget that! He doesn't know what he's missing by not going out with you!" Jess grinned at me, but she definitely had something on her mind, most likely Ian!

Once Mr Brookes had spoken to Roxie's prospective new owner, he returned to put us through our paces but the lady did not move.

"Oh boy!" sighed Jess, "She wants to see me put Roxie to the test. See you in hospital, Helen!"

"Knowing my luck!" I grimaced, looking down at Barney's flowing copper-coloured mane.

"Do we know anything about how these two jump?" I asked Roger Brookes, and he simply shook his head and grinned. For some reason I did not feel too optimistic.

Jess took Roxie up to the jumps first. Whatever the mare had liked in her past, jumping was clearly not in the mix. She took one look at the first, small jump and simply skidded to a halt, her hind legs almost catching up with her forelegs as she slid on the wet grass.

"Come again!" said her father. This was not going to be an easy exercise. Time and time again, Jess gently but firmly brought the mare round to the jumps. Time after time, Roxie took one look and backed off. Eventually, Roger Brookes had to admit that even a small jump was not going to work for Roxie. He changed it to a pole on the ground, then changed the coloured pole to a plain one when she shied away from that. Eventually, after about half an hour, Roxie finally stepped tentatively over the pole and we would have cheered, but for Roxie's nervous nature. Jess's father had her take the mare over that a few more times until she did so more calmly then he wisely asked her to stop and make a big fuss of her. Roxie's prospective new owner did not seem at all phased. In fact she looked fairly happy. Clearly Jess was right about her and she was so set on Roxie that nothing would put her off. It was good to see someone who clearly loved Roxie already and would no doubt give her a wonderful forever home.

It was my turn at last, and the wait had not made it any easier for me. I had been wondering what experience, if any, Barney had of jumping and I was about to find out whether I liked it or not.

First of all it seemed to be going smoothly. I very carefully eased the big horse into a steady canter and got him balanced and calm before turning him towards the three little jumps. That was when the whole mood changed. It was almost as if a switch had been flicked. Barney's ears pricked forward and his speed suddenly increased dramatically.

"Sit up! Sit back!" I heard Jess's father cry, but I had no time to do anything, no warning. All I could see was the hillside rushing towards me at a frightening speed as Barney surged forward. I sat back until the last moment, in case he was about to do what Roxie had done. However, on reaching the first jump, Barney simply launched himself into the air, making easy work of the small obstacle. No more time to think as he was already bearing down on the second, which disappeared beneath us. The third was even more effortless. I was so taken by surprise that I was not doing what a show jumper should do. I was not looking ahead to where I was going next. The jumping course may be finished but

Barney clearly was not. I could hear cries and yells in the distance but they were too far away. Suddenly my heart plummeted into my stomach as the post and rail fence of the paddock was much closer than I remembered it. I judged it to be between four and five feet high. Barney was running straight at it. Given his speed, I was in for a very nasty fall when he saw it and slammed the brakes on.

I had no choice now. I had to hang on for grim death as there was no time to try and stop Barney. I frantically wondered in those final seconds, how he was going to stop. He was sure to be injured too. I closed my eyes, waiting for the horrible, crunching impact….but it did not come. To my amazement I was suddenly and dramatically airborne. Unbelievably, Barney had taken off and cleared the huge paddock rail without putting a foot wrong. I had another problem now, the problem of finding a way to stop the big horse before he jumped over the next fence, and the next. I had to take a chance so I sat back and finally managed to turn his head so that he was forced to circle and slow down and eventually he gave in and came to a halt. The others were coming up the field towards me and I dismounted so that Barney could not take off with me again.

I wondered if Roger Brookes would be angry with me so I was surprised to see him actually grinning as he came towards me.

"Are you OK, Helen?" he asked me first, and I nodded, too breathless to reply. He seemed so very excited that I wondered if it should be me asking him that question!

"That was amazing!" he exclaimed, "Do you know that paddock rail is about four foot ten?" He jumped it like it was a pole on the ground. Don't you see what this means? This horse could find an owner much easier than we thought. That height was nothing to him - he could clear much higher. He's got a real talent for jumping and with his size he would do an adult rider for show jumping and cross country. If word got about that we had a possible jumping champion here, he could find his forever home." I nodded politely but for some reason I was less enthusiastic. I felt like I'd been on a very scary roller-coaster ride with no seatbelts provided. I glanced at Barney standing next to me, looking very pleased with himself. I reached into my pocket to find a carrot slice for him, but before I had the chance to get it out and feed it to him, he butted me with his head and I fell flat on my back on the grass, the breath knocked out of my body all over again!

## CHAPTER NINE

The next time I visited the stables I was amused to find that Mr Brookes had moved Barney to the paddock with the higher and more secure fences, with Buster for company, as he did not want the horse getting the idea that he could jump all the fences and escape the stables entirely. Now that he had the idea, he could clearly do it again. I shuddered just thinking about what could have happened had the big horse decided to make a bid for freedom.

I took a well-earned break from studying for the best part of a week just to concentrate on helping out the Brookes. Both Jess and myself had a wonderful week as we felt we brought Roxie and Barney on even more, and also managed to stay in the saddle while doing so. I felt more and more confident although I had to have my wits about me just in case Barney decided to pull a rodeo style stunt.

"You know, it's funny how things work out" Jess said, as she hung up Roxie's saddle, "When Heidi went and we had just Roxie and Barney to work with, I just assumed we wouldn't be riding them and that Dad would do most of the work. But now here we are. I have to say Roxie's by far the toughest horse I've ever ridden. What about you?"

"Me too!" I said, in turn hanging up Barney's big, heavy saddle on the bracket, "When I first saw Barney I just pictured a big man riding him and didn't think I'd be having anything to do with him, but to be honest he's surprised me. He's amazing!" Jess smiled. Everyone around here was still talking about *that* jump!

"When these two go, they'll take some living up to!" said Jess, and she then became quiet and thoughtful, "I'll kind of miss them in a way."

"Me too" I sighed, "But it's like your Dad says, the best you can hope for is for all of these horses to go to loving homes with people who're really prepared to do the work and take care of them. If I feel sad about any of them moving on, I just remind myself of that." I couldn't have sounded entirely convincing though, as Jess looked at me sideways and said,

"You're not over Heidi, are you?"

"No" I sighed again, "I'm not!"

Once again it was getting late and my mother was annoyed because Richard had not showed up for dinner. As always, I was sent to the garage to hurry him along.

"Oh no, is that the time?" Richard slid out from under a battered old white car, his face smudged with oil and grease, "Just give me a minute to clean up and I'll be over!" He disappeared to the back room to get cleaned up and I turned on my heel to leave, just as a familiar voice called,

"Hello Helen!" I turned back quickly and there was Derek, standing in his overalls with a spanner in his hand. He put the tool down and came over, "I was hoping to catch you." he continued, "Do you have a minute?" I nodded, "I just wanted to say, about meeting up for the cinema and getting fish and chips, are you still up for that?" I nodded, a little embarrassed and taken by surprise. "So, are you free tomorrow night?"

"Yes" I said, "I'm sure my French ink exercise can wait another day. Who else is all going?" Derek glanced behind him but there was no sign of Richard.

"Helen, there's something I need to say to you. I was hoping you'd take the hint but you haven't!"

"What are you trying to say, Derek?" I felt very strange all of a sudden, if I'm honest I felt a little weak at the knees!

"I'm trying to tell you I like you, Helen. I'm not talking about anyone else, I'm talking about you and me. I'm asking you out on a date!"

"A date? Me?" I echoed, wondering what he must be thinking of me. Derek was cool and calm and here I was, opening and closing my mouth like a dazed goldfish, repeating things parrot fashion and shaking so much that I could barely trust myself to stay upright.

"So what do you say? Are we on?"

"Yes! Yes of course we are!" I forced myself to say, as my limbs no longer seemed to be under my control. Just then, Richard came back in before we could finish our conversation. Derek must have been prepared for such an event, however, as he discreetly pushed a slip of paper into my hand. When I opened it up later, it suggested we met outside the cinema at 7.30 and included his phone number. He just gave me a little grin and I noticed a smudge of oil on the side of his nose. I thought about how much I would like to wipe it off…

"Are you sure you're OK, Helen?" my father looked up from his paper and stared at me curiously, "You seem to be on another planet tonight?"

"I haven't' noticed anything different" muttered Richard, who had his head in a motoring magazine, and I giggled almost hysterically. I loved making the tea and coffee after our meal and often did it, but I had never spooned sugar into the kettle before. I did not normally put tea and coffee in the same cup either. I really had surpassed myself. But how could I be calm and collected now? The guy I had a big crush on, the one and only gorgeous Derek Hall, had actually asked me out on a date! My first real date and it wasn't with a spotty, immature boy from school, it was with a mature, good looking young man who was already working. What more could a girl want?

I decided not to tell anyone that I was seeing Derek that evening. I didn't want gossip and I certainly did not want people reading too much into it, handing out the wedding invitations as Jess would have called it. I decided to play it cool. Having a secret from Samantha Inglis was a bonus, especially after her performance the other day. I was still angry with her as she had not just insulted me, she'd insulted Jess, Derek and Terry as well. I did not like to be smug as it did not suit me. I preferred to keep it to myself and be secretly smug. I was assuming nothing, though. I was only fourteen and still did not plan to tie myself to just the one man, even if it was the handsome Derek. I was still dedicated to the horses above all else. I so often heard about people who had given everything up when they had met the man or woman of their dreams but I was not like that. I would show everyone that my head would not be turned by a man, no matter how handsome or charming.

I could not eat or sleep the night before the date. Time seemed to go really slowly and I tried not to be too obviously looking at my watch. If anyone noticed my behaviour, they did not say so. I guessed that they must all consider it normal for me to behave oddly. Much as I disliked lying, I had convinced myself that what I told my parents was a necessary white lie. I told them I was going to Jess's this evening and they had no reason to disbelieve me. After all, it was my second home and I spent much of my time there. I had not even told Jess, so I had to hope against hope that they would not decide to call me at Jess's house. In turn I had told Jess that I was visiting relatives so that she would not phone looking for me.

I was calmer once I was with Derek. He was dressed in jeans, a denim jacket and a black T-shirt, his dark hair combed back and no oil or grease to be seen. He had obviously spent some time shaving, I thought, blushing slightly. He really looked very good and I felt proud to be seen with him. Here I was, plain old Helen, usually covered in mud, hay, and animal hair out with a handsome young man on a date! It was like something from one of those silly magazines which Jess sometimes read. I could hardly believe it was happening to me.

"Don't look so serious!" Derek grinned at me as we walked down to the local cinema, "It's not a tragedy we're going to see, it's a romantic comedy! And I'm sorry I'm not whisking you off in my posh car. I haven't earned enough yet even to buy an old banger, and we can't have a date pushing an old car, can we?" He looked at me with his large, dark brown eyes and I almost melted. I said nothing but to be honest I wouldn't have minded if we travelled by tractor!

We spent a pleasant evening seeing a romantic film, then Derek bought us fish and chips and he walked me home. I did not invite him into the house since I was supposed to be at Jess's. After saying goodnight to Derek, I felt a little anxious, worrying that the game might be up. However, back in the house all was quiet and the TV was on. There were no harsh words waiting for me. I seemed to have got away with it. Derek said he was going to contact me about another date, and I felt really good inside. I could not get him out of my head after that. I dreamed of him at night, dreamed that he was kissing me in some romantic tropical paradise…but then the alarm clock woke me up...

It was back to reality again at school. The headmaster was displeased by several things. Firstly he knew that pupils were smoking on school premises and warned, yet again, that there would be consequences. He was annoyed about the amount of litter being dropped in the school playground. He ended by handing round letters for our parents warning us all to be vigilant as attention had been drawn to two young men who were mugging people and robbing business premises. They had not got much so far but it seemed that they were also stalking and staking people out with a view to breaking into their homes. Aside from businesses, they had targeted mostly well-to-do people and households. They had attacked a convenience store in our district and there had been sightings here and there. Some witnesses said there was sometimes a third young man, possibly a getaway driver or a look out, although there were no definite sightings of a particular car. I stuffed the note into my bag just hoping that these crooks would not hit on me or my loved ones.

I had two more dates with Derek which really boosted my confidence but having lied several times now I took Jess into my confidence. She did not seem surprised and revealed that Derek had actually told her of his intention to ask me out! This explained all the knowing looks passing between them! Being so short of confidence, I had naturally assumed the two were an item! Having told Jess, I finally thought I had better tell my parents before they found out from someone else. I was apprehensive but one Friday after school, I decided to tell them before heading off to the stables.

However, it was my parents who ended up taking me by surprise. Richard was there as well, as he had a half day. They sat us down in the living room and there was a serious sense of expectation. Almost guiltily, I found myself hoping they were not about to tell us that we were going to have a baby brother or sister. Babies were definitely not my scene.

“We’ve got some good news for you” said our father, “It’s your mum who’s got the news so she’s going to tell you.” our mother was not just smiling, she was positively beaming,

“I’ve found a job!” she said, “I didn’t want to tell you I’d been looking. It’s so long since I last worked that I thought no one would take me on. It’s nothing world shattering, just working in the office at an accountancy firm. I haven’t worked since Richard was a baby. We’ll see how it goes from here.” They had bought some more expensive food than usual for dinner to celebrate and this certainly caught me off guard. It was our father who was in and out of work, and always looking for something. I had almost forgotten that our mother was clever and had been studying for a psychology degree just before Richard’s birth! Money had been the reason she sadly had to give it up. She was the one who was always around to look after us while school friends’ parents were often out working. In some households both parents were out working, and I often wondered if that was what made Samantha Inglis such a pain!

With this happy mood in the house, I felt it was all right to share my news too.

"A boyfriend?" said my mother, as she slid a delicious slice of lemon pie onto my plate, "It's not Andy, is it?"

"You're on the right lines, Mum, it's someone who works at the garage. Derek Hall."

"Oh yes, you've been talking quite a lot about him, you know. Even more than the horses! We'll have to meet him sometime. He can come round for a meal some day. Just arrange it with him."

"So I take it you want to check him out!" I joked.

"No, not at all. But you said he was good looking so I just want to make sure that's true!" we all laughed. I felt so relieved as it had been so much easier than expected, and now the good news about our mother's new job. Could it be that things were finally looking up?

## CHAPTER TEN

"It's just not like you to fail your Latin translation, Helen" Mr Carling was a very good teacher and could even be quite strict, but on the whole he was kind-hearted. He had discreetly kept me back after class, rather than embarrassing me in front of all my classmates, and was now sitting on the edge of his desk, looking over his glasses at me with concern in his eyes, "I don't want to pry, but if anything's bothering you, it will go no further, and if you don't want to tell me, you could tell another teacher instead. We don't want anyone to suffer alone."

"Thanks" I said, "But actually, it's nothing bad. It's just that so much is happening with my mum getting a new job and that's changed a lot around the house. I've been helping more at home and I've been spending a lot of time at the stables. I'm really sorry, I *will* knuckle down, I promise."

I was lucky, I thought, as I hurried away after that encounter. Another teacher would just have shouted me down in front of everyone and I'd have been teased afterwards. It was partly the truth, but my main problem was that any time I sat down to do my homework or revision now, I hadn't got very far when an image of Derek Hall would swim into my mind, his smile, his laughter, the ridiculous jokes he told, , his finely tuned body and powerful build, the sweep of his dark, glossy hair….I snapped out of it, realising it was happening again. I was angry with myself. After all, wasn't I always teasing Jess and some of the other girls over believing what they read in girlie magazines, how to kiss properly, how to do your lipstick properly, or how to win over that boy in your class you really like….as if? Yet here I was, besotted with Derek Hall after knowing him for so short a time. I just couldn't help myself. And, to my shame, I wasn't even thinking so much about the horses now!

I decided enough was enough. I had no arrangement with Derek tonight. After dinner I went up to my room for an hour, and studied as much Latin as I could realistically assimilate. I felt much more relaxed, and relieved, as I lay back on my bed for a few minutes, just looking around my room. Pictures and photos of horses everywhere. Drawings I had done, some of them from years back. Many photos of me with Heidi, me with Jess and the horses and, more recently, a few photos of Barney.

I changed my clothes and went straight to the stables. Jess was there but not alone. I was somewhat taken aback to see another girl from school, Elaine Barker, also dressed in riding clothes.

"Oh hello, Helen" said Jess, "Are you joining us?"

"Well, that was the plan" I said, "Hello there Elaine. Are you riding tonight?" Elaine nodded, "You're not riding Barney, are you?" Elaine laughed and shook her head,

"No, I'm riding Minx. I take it that you're riding Barney then? There don't seem to be many volunteers!"

We just rode round the fields in the area and let the horses relax a bit. Roxie was definitely going better for Jess, so much calmer and less jumpy than I had ever seen her, in fact. She was also back to her full fitness and had gained just enough weight to make her look really fit and healthy, just as Barney was now. He was so much bigger than I had first thought, however, and he seemed even larger when I was on his back.

Once the ride was over and we had returned the horses to their fields, I turned to Jess as we were hanging up the saddles and bridles,

“So this person who’s interested in Roxie, is she still interested?” I asked, once again struggling to put Barney’s saddle on the bracket due to its weight.

“Wendy? Yes she is, but she’s in the middle of moving house, the place she’s moving to has the stables and everything. Dad says it’s OK and he wont’ sell her to anyone else while she gets sorted, but at least I get to ride Roxie for a few more weeks. I’m quite attached now! Not in love with her but she really is sweet and she’s got a lot of talent, just been badly treated I guess. Barney as well, he’s really coming on.”

“Has there been any interest in Barney though?” I wondered, but Jess simply shrugged and shook her head.

“Dylan will soon be ready for action though” Jess said, “So the plan is that I’ll swap to him once he’s fully recovered and Roxie goes.” I nodded. Jess looked at me strangely, as if she was about to say something else, but then thought better of it and stopped herself. I thought no more of it.

It was a Thursday morning only a week or so from my fifteenth birthday. As I approached the shops and bus stop, I knew at once all was not well. There were three Police cars and an ambulance outside Gail's shop. I wanted to know what was going on but of course the Police officers were preventing people from going in, and seeing those before us turned away, we decided not to bother trying. There were quite a number of school pupils waiting for the bus and one of the officers asked us to stand back, saying it was all under control. Just then, clanking and grinding sounds announced the arrival of Terry's bus, so we were none the wiser.

However, the rumour mill sprang to life as always.

"It's those boys" Samantha Inglis was annoying that way, always seeming to have the news before anyone else, "The ones we got a letter about. They mugged someone or held the place up with shotguns or something. They're saying someone died."

I tended to take Samantha's comments with a pinch of salt as she loved to over-dramatise everything so that she could be the centre of attention. Facts slowly leaked out though. Gail's shop remained closed for a few days but there was an announcement at the school assembly. Apparently two youths had held up the shop and terrorised customers, pushing one of them to the floor in the process. They got the money from the till and fled. No serious injuries but some shock, especially for Gail. It could have been so much worse but we had to be extra careful now. Some people said they saw two youths, but they had woolly hats on their heads so they were not easy to identify as they were wearing dull coloured clothes also. Other witnesses said there was a third youth who was the look out, dressed similarly and behaving suspiciously outside the premises. The attacks were getting closer to home.

"I'm so sorry, Barney" I sighed into the big horse's long, flame-coloured mane that evening as I gave him a thorough grooming out in the yard, "I've been neglecting you, haven't I? If you stand still and be a good boy for me, you might even get some sugar and you're not really meant to have that, you know!" I kissed him gently on the nose, and as if understanding every word, Barney gave an enormous sigh and nudged my shoulder which made me laugh. The horses certainly had a way of making me feel better when things were difficult.

Despite my best efforts, it seemed that everyone knew about me and Derek now. A few people had tried to warn me, saying he was too old for me and other advice, but I knew myself best and a few years was nothing. It was not as if I was planning to marry Derek; he was my boyfriend but there were no wedding arrangements made. While I just wanted to go with the flow, however, my mind had a way of trying to make me look forward, seeing myself marrying Derek and having his children. I'd been out with him six times and I wasn't even fifteen! I really had to get my feet back on the ground and keep things in perspective.

So I tried, hard as it was at the age of fourteen, to put things into compartments. I helped prepare the meals, went to school and worked hard, studied and did my homework on specific days of the week, saw Derek two evenings a week and went to the stables the rest of the time. As time went by, Derek wanted to see me at weekends as well. Despite myself, I ended up agreeing to this. The way I felt right now, if he'd asked for my hand in marriage I would have said yes, even though I was fourteen years old. I really had fallen head over heels.

"I never realised being with you would be this good" Derek looked directly into my eyes as we sat facing each other in Capaldi's Cafe on the Saturday before my birthday, "I'd like you to be my steady girlfriend. Would you like that?" He stroked my hand gently.

"Of course I would" I sighed, looking into his deep, expressive brown eyes, "I don't have room for any other guys in my life, and let's face it, none of them are remotely interested in me anyway!"

"I know someone who is!" said Derek, with a grin.

"And who might that be?"

"Barney of course!" we both giggled, but that soon changed, as Derek leaned forward and took me in his arms, kissing me more passionately than ever before. Part of me wanted to run off because I was worried about being too young and getting involved, but I was already involved…

Almost every time I went to the stables, Elaine Barker was there. Jess was talking to her a lot at school too, and they were spending more and more time together. I was annoyed with myself for feeling irritated with them, but I couldn't help myself. Jess and I had always been really close, like sisters. People did change, something I had learned as I grew from childhood to adulthood but it did make me wonder if something was wrong.

I did ask her, but when I did, she told me everything was fine and there was nothing wrong with our friendship. This was almost more annoying. In some ways it would have been preferable if she'd told me she no longer liked me! There was no law against her being friendly with Elaine. I was friendly with a few others too, but what I had with Jess was very special, at least I had always thought so...

However, it all came to a head one day in the English class when we had been asked to work in pairs. I immediately turned to Jess, only to find that she already had Elaine by her side and they were poring over a book.

I worked with another girl but felt very hurt. What had I done wrong, I wondered?

Later on, when Jess sat next to Elaine on the bus yet again, I decided to confront her as we walked home.

Elaine got off at a different bus stop so we did not walk home with her normally.

"Look Jess" I said, as we consumed our sweets from Gail, who was none the worse for her scare, "I need to know now, is there something wrong? We used to do everything together, now we don't!"

Jess stopped under a tree, opened her bag, dropped the package of sweets into it, then turned to me, somewhat hesitantly.

"If you want the honest truth, Helen, we used to be so close because we had so much in common. We did everything together, but you've *changed!* I just can't believe how much! We agreed to share everything together and do everything together but now you're at the yard less and less. I don't understand why because you swore you were dedicated to horses! And you should hear yourself these days, it's Derek this, Derek that! After all that stuff you said about soppy boyfriend stories in magazines, Helen, you're the one who's out there being all soppy, snogging him and flaunting him for the whole world to see!" I was momentarily silent as what she had said was a total shock to me. I'd had no idea at all.

"Are you jealous?" I ventured.

"Jealous? You've got me all wrong, Helen, and I thought we knew each other! I told you I don't fancy Derek, that he's not my type, and that's completely true. When we spent a bit of time together, he asked if you were going out with anyone and other questions about you. Not me. You. I'm not jealous, in fact I like Derek and I'm happy that you seem to have found someone, but….I just want the old Helen back!" I felt very strange all of a sudden. There I was thinking that Jess may be angry or jealous, when in fact she was just feeling hurt and left out!

"I'm so sorry, Jess! I had no idea I was doing that! So, is our friendship really over?" I looked at my best friend helplessly. I was surprised to see that Jess looked close to tears, but she quickly turned on her heel and over her shoulder she said,

"Only if you want it to be, Helen."

I remained under the tree for a good few more minutes, thinking over what Jess had just said. Was it true? Had I become this monster since I started dating Derek? Did I really talk of nothing but him and show him off like a prize winning show dog? It was certainly true that my school work *had* suffered, and true that my unwavering commitment to horses *was* dwindling. But was it meant to be like that? Throwing away my goals, messing up my school work and losing lifelong friends? Was this what romance was about?

I did not mention anything to Derek, and we continued to date. Things were becoming more difficult with Jess and as a result, I started to go to the stables less often. I felt terrible though, because I knew that even if Elaine Barker was there every day, she would ride Minx or Buster and poor Barney would just be kicking his heels, literally, as no one else was likely to climb on board. While I didn't want to take my spite out by neglecting this lovely horse, I did not want more any more confrontations with Jess, who was now stuck to Elaine like glue, and making me feel foolish more and more often. I had a dilemma. I had good things in my life, my mother had a new job, I was doing very well with helping to train Barney, and I had a boyfriend who I really liked, but I now found myself in this very unpleasant situation. Which way should I turn?

I couldn't even have Terry as a shoulder to cry on - he was not going to be on the school run for two weeks, as he was driving the service bus which went into Glasgow. All I could do was wave if I saw him when I was out and about. He was just a good person to talk to, very calm and wise, even if Samantha Inglis was jealous and called me a brazen hussy who flirted with bus drivers!

I would normally involve Jess in my birthday celebrations but not this year. It was embarrassing and it was in fact Derek who saved the day by suggesting the two of us went out and saw a film, followed by a meal. I really did enjoy myself and felt very special. It made me feel so much better than I had done in years, especially as Derek kept telling me that I was his special girl and he had never felt this way about anyone before. It was all so new and exciting...

However, when it was over and I came home to find a little card and parcel waiting for me, I felt quite sad,

"Jess dropped this off for you" my mother said, glancing at me a little curiously, "Is there anything you want to tell me, Helen, I mean about you and Jess?"

That was it. At first I stuttered and stammered, but then I just burst into tears and it all came out. I was making so much noise that Richard came down from his bedroom to see what all the fuss was about. My mother just held me in her arms as I sobbed for what seemed like hours.

"I've messed up!" I kept repeating over and over again, "I'm an idiot! I had so much going for me and now I've sacrificed it all because of a guy! I guess I was just greedy thinking I could have friends, work with the horses *and* have a boyfriend! I didn't realise I had to choose between them!"

"You don't necessarily have to choose between them" said Mum, always calm whatever the situation, "But sometimes other people don't behave the way we expect them to. The different things in your life can be at odds with each other. You know how you balance your school work with the horses? Well, you need to do that with your friends. Having a boyfriend can just take over, you're tempted to spend every free minute with him. You may not see it this way but if you try and balance everything out, you'll be much healthier. Let Derek wait, don't let him think you're at his beck and call. I'm sure he'll understand if you want to spend time with Jess, and the horses too. If he doesn't understand that, he isn't worth having as a friend or boyfriend."

I did not take much in at that time, but I did think many times about the words my mother had said to me. She had lived longer than me and had more life experience so she did know what she was talking about. I just felt so bad because I hadn't realised how it seemed to Jess. I knew I needed to make it up to her, but how?

## CHAPTER ELEVEN

It was another wet day, and I had been hoping for a nice Saturday to spend a lot of time at the stables. However, I shrugged on my rain wear and decided to make the most. Derek had told me he was busy with his parents this weekend so we wouldn't see each other until Monday evening. This gave me a bit of breathing space and much-needed time with the horses.

The stable yard was bustling when I arrived. A large horse box was parked in the centre of the yard and as I approached, Jess came out of the stables leading Roxie who was wearing a rug and protective bandages for travelling. Jess gave me a weak grin as I came up and gave her a hug. Wendy, the lady who was buying the mare was standing there in her rain wear too, and I suddenly really felt for Jess. I realised that, even though she had her own horse to love and care for, she too felt the pain when the really special ones left. They were all of course special in their way but there were just one or two with whom we formed special bonds. Jess stood with Roxie beside her for a moment, as if trying to regain her composure, then she flung her arms round the mare's neck and gave her a huge hug, something the nervous animal would not have tolerated just a few weeks ago. I was both happy and sad. Happy that Roxie had found her forever home against the odds, but sad that her time here was over and sad for Jess, too.

Hugging Jess was a great release, as there were still tensions between us. The situation with Derek was still ongoing although I had been better organised and made sure I spent more time doing my homework as well as with the horses. Despite my urge to talk about him non-stop, I did my best to bite my tongue and discuss a variety of topics. I felt better, but Jess and I were not quite back to where we had been. I was worried that it may never be the same between us. I still felt torn as I wanted to spend time with Derek, the man who I had fallen in love with despite myself.

My thoughts were interrupted by a loud neigh. Turning, I saw Mary Rose, Barney, Buster and Minx at the field gate, all of their ears pricked forward with interest. The ear-shattering greeting had of course come from Barney who was practically dancing on the spot with excitement. I had to laugh as they all looked so comical standing in a row.

With that, Roger Brookes helped Wendy to close up the horse box and they shook hands. Wendy looked at Jess, obviously conscious of her distress, and then came over and gave her a little hug before getting into the cab and driving slowly out of the yard, taking Roxie to her new home, and out of our lives forever.

"She's going way up north" said Jess, her voice catching, "So it's not as if we're going to bump into her."

"She'll be good, Jess, you can see how much Wendy loves her" I sighed, "I got like this with Beauty and

Heidi, that's why I have to force myself never to get like this again."

"You're human, girls, that's all." Roger Brookes had clearly overheard, "There's no use trying to force yourself not to fall in love with horses, because you'll always get one or two who get you that way. I know I've tried to warn you but I know it's hard but go with the flow. Don't try to stop your feelings because that'll make it worse. Don't worry, Jess, there's plenty of work for you. Dylan's all yours at least for the time being and he's certainly a lot quieter to handle than Roxie was, so it'll be easier." Jess and I both nodded, but neither of us convincingly. As Jess passed the stable which had housed Roxie over summer, she slowly and quietly peeled off the temporary sticker with the horse's name on it, always a reminder of a horse who was just passing through, and probably the next horse's name would appear on a sticker there fairly soon.

"Oh and girls" Roger said as he turned to leave us, "Forgot to mention, I managed to spread around Barney's reputation a bit more, you know, the fact he's got a great natural jump in him. Well, there's a man interested in coming to try him out on Tuesday."

The rain had lessened slightly. Jess and I brought in Barney and Mary Rose and got them ready in silence. I was not sure what was wrong with me. I seemed to be feeling more despondent about Roxie moving on than I had first realised. It was a changing of the guard. Roxie was gone and it was now highly possible that Barney would also be moving on shortly. In truth we'd had an unexpectedly wonderful summer with both horses. We had never imagined it would be this good. We'd naturally assumed neither of us would connect with these two seemingly unsuitable mounts, or certainly unsuitable for two slight teenage girls. However, we had been wrong in the nicest possible way. It had actually been a lot of fun!

We took the horses over some jumps but kept them low as we did not want to risk any slipping or sliding which could cause injury. Barney was on top form again and as before I felt that he could jump much higher if he was asked. It now seemed that a man would be coming to try him out and would probably buy him. Barney had come on a lot from the rangy, undisciplined animal which had first arrived. One thing in his favour was his gentle, amicable nature. He was very comical somehow, as if he had a human streak and could work out and even react to our moods. He seemed to be on our wavelength as if understanding our conversations. One thing was certain - I would miss him.

Later on, Jess's parents gave us both some money to go to the cinema and get chips as they felt we needed it due to all the big changes going on. We'd been through a lot and really appreciated it.

We had a lovely evening. The rain cleared away and although it was not warm, at least we didn't have to rush home huddled under umbrellas.

"I feel better already!" laughed Jess, "I love the romantic films, even if I'll never end up snogging Ian that way!"

"Knowing horses, you'd have to snog Marmaduke Jinx as well!" I laughed, and we both giggled.

As we turned the corner near the shop, a sudden movement in the hedgerow made me jump. Thinking it was just a nocturnal animal in the undergrowth, I carried on walking, but then, all hell broke loose. Someone grabbed me strongly by the shoulders, pushing me roughly to the cold, wet ground. I struggled and tried to scream but I was overpowered and something was roughly shoved over my mouth to keep me quiet. I heard Jess screaming somewhere and felt my shoulder bag being ripped away from me. There was nothing I could do. I heard voices I did not recognise, male voices. I kept struggling although it was clearly futile. My attacker's grip was extremely powerful.

"Get the other one!" muttered a gruff, unfamiliar voice. I had by now realised that we were under attack and we were being robbed. I did not have much time to think of anything else. I knew I had to get away. I knew they could hurt us as well. I tried kicking but it felt like someone was sitting on me. I felt the hard ground chilling my bones, the dampness seeping through my clothes. Through the madness, I thought that I heard the sound of an engine. Was that the getaway car? Maybe we were going to be kidnapped. Suddenly, a vaguely familiar male voice shouted,

"Stop that! Hold it right there! You! Come here!" The weight was suddenly and abruptly lifted from me. In my confused state I did not know how many people had just showed up but a woman's voice in the background said she was going to call the Police.

"Helen! Are you OK? Helen?" I was astonished to find myself looking into the worried, freckled face of Terry the bus driver.

"Terry?" I was confused, "Where did you come from?"

"I was working - I drive this route, Helen, just as well I do! Don't worry about these guys. It's all over! Now, are you hurt? Can you get up?" Terry helped me stagger to my feet. I was bruised and shaken, but no serious damage from what I could tell. I was still stunned and overwhelmed with so many emotions that I just fell into his arms and sobbed.

"Jess!" I suddenly panicked, "Where's Jess?"

"All right" Terry held me close, patting my shoulder, "Some of the neighbours came out too, she's with them - she's OK."

I glanced round and saw that three sheepish looking youths were sitting on the wall with two burly men, presumably Terry's bus passengers, guarding them. They had their heads bowed, and were well covered by woolly hats. I did not even feel anger towards them as I was still stunned. I saw Jess then, and she gave me a watery grin. Gail from the shop was there with her as she had obviously heard the disturbance and come out. However, there was something else, something which had not been said, something in Jess's eyes, and when I looked back at Terry, the same look was in his eyes. Something was wrong. They both seemed to know what it was but it was being kept from me.

Before I had a chance to try and find out, the Police arrived and the questioning began.

"Yes we got all three" I heard Terry saying, "I was lucky to have help from some passengers on the bus."

Jess finally came to stand beside me when our individual questioning was over.

"The three of them have been arrested and they'll be taken into custody." one of the officers was saying. I glanced at Jess and she gave me a pained look. Terry came back over and both of them looked at each other, then at me.

"Is something wrong?" I said, exasperated.

Still, nothing was said, but Jess put her arm round me, and I realised she was leading me to the Police car. I looked back at Terry questioningly but he just nodded soberly, as if he knew what was coming.

We arrived just as two officers were leading the third suspect to the car, handcuffed and stripped of his woolly hat.

"I didn't mean it! They made me do it!" the young man protested, and I suddenly realised his voice was familiar. Suddenly, I felt seriously confused. Just before reaching the car, the dark-haired young man turned his head and I saw him properly. I did not want to believe, did not want to see, and I had to look away. The third suspect was Derek Hall.

"Stupid, stupid fool!" I cried, howled and punched my pillow. My eyes were red, sore and tired from crying. How could I have been so dumb? It seemed that my ideal boyfriend had been using me as a way of trying to gain access to the Brookes' house and possibly their business too. I was of no further use except as a way of leading them to Jess. I had been told that the only stupid ones were the youths themselves, preying on people and businesses often in broad daylight and on youngsters who would not have very much money as a rule. It was a cowardly way of trying to gain access to some of the more affluent residences in the area. They had been branded cowards and other things but I was the one left feeling as stupid and empty-handed as the thieves themselves.

"You weren't to know!" my mother said the next day at dinner, "He had us all fooled. We thought he was a nice guy as well, seemed to really like you. In fact maybe that part wasn't an act after all."

I wanted to think that, wanted to believe that Helen Doyle, the ugly duckling, was capable of attracting a handsome date just for being herself, but probably that was too much to ask and I was back to square one. I could now dedicate my time to my studies and the horses equally, be free to help with whatever new horse or horses Roger Brookes happened to be getting in. But it was a hopeless, hollow feeling all the same.

I arrived at the Brookes' place and as I always did, I went down to the stables first, to check if anyone was there. If not, I would go up to the house. The first horse I saw was Dylan, now out in the field with the others. Further up the field, I saw the other horses grazing. There was no sign of Jess and her father, or even Lizzie the Beagle. It was very quiet.

I glanced up and down the field at the lovely, peaceful scene and just tried to wish myself back a few weeks. Just a few weeks ago it had been my fifteenth birthday. I had a boyfriend, a good relationship with my best friend, kept up with my school work and was doing well with the horses. Now it all seemed to be gone. My boyfriend was a crook, the horses we'd had over summer were all but gone, and my relationship with Jess may be strained forever. Elaine Barker did seem to have receded though. She was not a keen rider like we were, and a fall from Buster, albeit a minor one, seemed to have put her off for good.

Despite myself, despite my resolve to move on, to get back on track, it was still too early. In that quiet place with no one around me and even the horses just disant shapes along the treeline, I sank my head into my hands and burst into tears, leaning on the five bar gate. I didn't know how long I sobbed for. I did not want to cry in front of Jess or her family, so I just let it all out, all the pent up worry, grief, disappointment and hollow emptiness inside.

Suddenly, unexpectedly, someone gently touched my shoulder. Without opening my eyes, I just leaned back into it, expecting to be asked why I was crying. But no one spoke. Before I could turn, there was a huge snort of breath right in my ear, and a wet, slobbery tongue licked my neck as I was pushed almost to the ground.

"Barney!" I grabbed the gate breathlessly, taken completely unaware. I was looking right into the chestnut horse's big, gentle eyes. He simply looked back at me and then he leaned his big head on my shoulder and remained there.

"Oh Barney!" I sobbed all over again, "Why did I trust him? Why did I let it happen and almost throw all this away for a guy who was just using me? Why? I'm not attractive to men after all. I'll never fit in. I'm a misfit, just like you!" It was oddly comforting to unload my grief onto someone who was never going to respond. When I did regain my composure a little, I looked and saw that the other horses were still up at the treeline, still grazing. Barney was the only one who had left them and come to me. Was he just looking for food or did he truly realise that I was in need of some comfort?

I had been in denial for so long. I was often in denial I had to admit - it was my way of trying to deal with possibly troublesome things. However, this was something I did not want to even entertain, due to what had happened in the past. Slowly but surely, against all the odds, I had fallen head over heels in love with Barney.

# CHAPTER TWELVE

"Have you seen your pictures in the paper?" my mother swept round to my place at the table to show me what I had already had in abundance at school all day, a photo of myself with Jess, Terry and a few other people, followed by a detailed report of all the drama which had unfolded in our town that fateful night.

"Hero bus driver Terry Stillman, twenty three, is to be honoured in a private ceremony at his workplace for his brave actions when he came to the aid of two Braepark High School girls who were under attack…." my mother was reading it out but I had heard it all before and was feeling quite overwhelmed. We had been invited to the ceremony for Terry and while I was looking forward to it, I really could have done with some time to myself to think and come to terms with the fact that my supposedly amazing love life was one massive lie. Also, the horse I had just admitted to loving was likely to be going very soon, and if not with this potential owner, then someone else who was sure to want Barney. What horse lover would not want Barney?

"I didn't even know his last name, Mum, he was always just Terry to me and I didn't even know he was twenty three."

"Too old for you, and now all the girls will be after him because he's a hero!" my mother replied, smiling at me, "Quite a looker, though, I have to say!"

"Ha ha" I said, "Me and Terry? You sound just like Samantha Inglis, *just a bus driver, very common and always in the pub and the bookies!"*

"You know that's not what I meant" said Mum, but we were both smiling.

The ceremony for Terry was not anything official, although he would of course be put forward for a citizenship award or something like that, I was told. They were just having a special thank you lunch at the bus depot, not even any alcohol to drink as it was during working hours. Jess and I were honoured to be there, with our parents and some of the others who had helped out.

I glanced at Jess. She was still subdued, and I wondered if it was from the attack itself or the impact of losing Roxie, which seemed to have hit her harder than I had expected. As for the effects of the attack on me, I had very mixed feelings right now. In all honesty, the shocking revelations about Derek and the impending loss of Barney were a much heavier weight on my mind than the assault. Yet I couldn't even begin to explain that to the people who surrounded me now. It might make me sound ungrateful for being rescued by Terry.

After the speeches, which were mercifully short, a blushing Terry posed for a few photos and Jess and I were included in some of them too. Cups of tea and coffee were handed round and we managed to find some biscuits before they disappeared. Everyone seemed to want a piece of Terry right now and I almost felt sorry for him. He had always struck me as a modest person who just worked quietly away and didn't draw attention to himself.

Eventually, when things had died down, I found myself standing next to him.

"How does it feel to be a hero?" I asked, half jokingly.

"To be honest, a bit embarrassing!" sighed Terry, placing his empty coffee cup on a nearby table, "I did what anyone would have done. I just happened to be driving along and saw that happening, didn't even realise it was you two."

"But you did stop, and you did save us" I said, "They could have killed us, they could have done anything, but you stopped them. You *are* a hero Terry, whether you like it or not! You're *my* hero!" I at once felt rather foolish about my choice of words, as it sounded like something out of one of those trashy novels I was always berating.

Terry was quiet for a while, which was unlike him, then he went on,

"I'm sorry about your boyfriend, I had no idea when a couple of us stopped him running off that it was him! It was Jess who realised. I knew you were seeing him so that's got to be a blow for you. Did you really like him?" he sounded genuinely concerned.

"Yes" I sighed, gazing at the floor, "I did. I was taken in and all I've got are people telling me I'm young and wasn't to know and I'll find someone else."

"Oh don't worry, I won't say that" said Terry with a grin, "But what I will say Helen, is this. Sometimes we're out there looking for the perfect life – perfect job, perfect relationship, perfect home or whatever. I know you can't wait to get to school leaving age so that you can go out in the world but in all honesty it may not be all it's cracked up to be."

"Meaning?"

"Meaning, I'm twenty three years old and I do have a job but just like you I live with Mum and Dad and they tell me off for having a messy room or not doing the dishes. Half these people didn't even notice me until I did what I did. I drive you guys to school and back most days and when I'm not, I'm on a service route through the town every day. Yet to them I'm just a bus driver. No one special. I heard that girl from your class saying that bus drivers go to the bookies and the pubs or whatever. I don't but that's not the point. I'm a bus driver so I'm circling the drain! You're different, Helen. You don't judge people by what job they do or what they earn. You see people as people, that's all."

"What point are you making, Terry? You and me?" I giggled.

“Of course not Helen!” grinned Terry, “You’re a great girl, but no, I’m not trying to seduce you or anything like that. What I’m trying to say is that sometimes all you want, all you’re ever looking for has always been right there in front of you.”

“I’m sorry, darling” my father ran his hands through his hair with a heavy sigh as we faced each other across the scratched old dining room table, “I just don’t see any way. You’ve had this problem so often, falling in love with Roger Brookes’ horses and then crying when they go. It’s a part of life, love, I’m sorry. We just can’t afford to buy you a horse. It’s all the upkeep as well. I would if I could, you know that.”

“But Barney’s special!” I sighed, “We have a bond. I told you how he comforted me when I was crying over Derek. And even the way he looks at me sometimes, as if he understands. He’s had a tough start in life and deserves a loving owner.”

“I do know, darling, and I’m sure he’s a great horse but your mum hasn’t been in her new job long enough to start spending that kind of money. You’ll just have to try and get over him like you did the others and hopefully another horse will come along that you like, and just have to try and hope things will change. You’re over Heidi now, aren’t you? Not so long ago you were crying into your pillow over her.”

I said nothing, as there was nothing I could say. Not any more. My father was right and I had already known before I started to plead my case that it was impossible. I had not wanted to be around when Barney's prospective new owner came to give him what we called a "test drive" but I changed my mind. The time was close so I quickly went to change my clothes so that I could make it in time. I had never seen anyone else ride Barney, so part of me was curious as to how this man, who was reputedly a highly skilled rider, would take to him. He would probably be a far better rider than I was, I thought glumly.

When I arrived at One Tree Farm, I was surprised to find the yard untidy, Lizzie the Beagle rushing around with a grooming brush in her jaws, and someone shouting in the distance. I curiously followed the raised voices, which seemed to be coming from the stable yard. Very strange. I had expected to see a scene of business being conducted and perhaps Roger Brookes discussing the sale with the new owner by now. Curious, I hurried to the main yard.

As I rounded the corner, I was astonished at the sight before my eyes. There in front of me was a large man dressed in what had obviously once been very expensive riding clothes. However, they were now covered from top to toe in black, sticky mud, looking like something from a comedy sketch. He was also irate, looming over Roger Brookes in a threatening manner while Roger tried, albeit unsuccessfully, to calm him down.

"I can't believe you tried to advertise this thing as a potential eventer and show jumper. You never mentioned it was off its head!" It was then I noticed over my shoulder that Barney, also covered in mud and still wearing his saddle and bridle, was grazing unconcerned in the field, with Jess in the background looking on in shocked silence.

"I told you this was a young and unpredictable horse" said Roger Brookes, "You should know that yourself, there's definitely potential in this horse."

"Potential to kill someone, maybe!" snarled the red-faced man, his eyes bulging menacingly. He really was big and quite frightening. I had not been in time to see anything happening but presumed he had hit the deck in a most undignified fashion! I secretly wished I *had* witnessed this and suppressed a giggle, quickly looking the other way. However, it hit me that the eventual loss of Barney was still looming in front of me and that was no laughing matter. My chuckle seemed to die away inside me as I contemplated that bleak fate.

Eventually, the man stormed off, got into the driving seat of an expensive looking car, mud and all, and roared off, spraying us with muck from the yard puddles. Jess, Roger Brookes and I all looked at each other and burst out laughing.

"Don't worry about that one" said Mr Brookes, trying to look serious but failing miserably, "Let's just say Barney didn't take to him!"

“Took *off* with him, more like!” giggled Jess, almost hysterical, “He was just so full of himself, the world’s number one rider! I didn’t like him at all so it was kind of funny!”

“Jess!” her father scolded, but he was laughing too, “I’m sure the right person will come along one day.”

So, a reprieve. But for how long?

## CHAPTER THIRTEEN

I could think of nothing but Barney. My friend, my ally, my comfort, my fire horse. I recalled the day when I first met him, not knowing his name and giving him fantasy names to do with fire and flames. He had bloomed into a fit, handsome young horse with so much ahead of him. I just wished I could find a way to keep him forever. I may be an optimist, but even so, some things were probably just a bridge too far. I may be young but I was old enough to know only too well that money did not grow on trees. Sadly, my father was correct. We simply did not, and may never have the means to buy me the horse of my dreams.

My school work suffered even more when Jess told me that a few people had been asking about Barney and someone else was thinking of trying him out now that her father had spread the word of his natural jumping skills. I tried to put a brave face on it but in the end I just bit my lip and looked away, as there really was nothing more I could say that would make any difference now. I just had to hope that I could make at least some headway with my school work before the teachers approached my parents to tell them how lazy and distracted I had become lately.

"Don't say anything" Jess sighed, "You don't have to say it. I know you love him, you can't hide it. I was the same with Roxie. Crazy, because I've got Mary Rose, my very own horse. Greedy girl, but I just couldn't help it. I felt so guilty admitting that when you're clearly so cut up about Barney and don't have your own horse like I do. I just felt for Roxie from day one, she was so scared and goodness only knows what had happened to her. She seemed so unsuitable for me but in the end I loved her, like you and Barney. Misfits, all of us."

I said nothing but the pain seeped through me like rain through an arid desert. I could not face losing Barney for good, not seeing his cheeky face looking at me over the stable door or field gate. Not being licked on the back of the neck, or slobbered over, or even knocked flat when the big horse decided to give me a friendly nudge. How could I face life without that? Worse still, how could I possibly have spent so many weeks hoping someone would buy him and Roxie so that they would both move on and we could hope for more suitable mounts to appear? Barney had inexplicably become that mount and I'd gone from almost wishing him away to wishing he would be mine forever!

School was over and after being dropped off by Terry and collecting our usual sweets, Jess and I headed over to her place to make the most. The nights were drawing in so we had to get our riding done before the daylight faded and that did not give us a great deal of time.

However, I was in for another shock. As we arrived at the stables, Roger Brookes was already there, and my heart sank way down to my boots when I saw what he was doing. He was removing the temporary sticker from the door of Barney's stable. Fingers of ice caressed my spine and my heart seemed to plunge even further as I recalled that day, very recently, when Jess had done that same thing with Roxie's sticker, almost in slow motion. I knew what it meant.

"Oh there you are, girls" he said. Jess just looked at him and I knew that it would be one of those looks to say "Poor Helen." I just had to ignore that now. I didn't want anyone's pity.

"Should I ride Buster?" I ventured, "If Barney's…." I couldn't say it, as I was really biting my lip now, fighting hard not to burst into tears.

"No Helen, you ride Barney- he's going nowhere just now" said Roger Brookes, "But you'd better be quick, it looks like rain."

Tears streamed down my face as I rode Barney in the field with Jess on Mary Rose. Jess and I did not speak much. I ended up quite glad of the rain when it finally did arrive, as my tears would be less noticeable, hopefully.

"My Mum and Dad have suggested an honorary dinner to celebrate the gang being caught and a few things like that, going to invite Terry as well, he deserves it! Of course if Samantha finds out she'll be going on about how illegal it is, you and an *older man!*"

"Ha ha! Very funny! But yes, Terry told me his Mum's a rubbish cook, so it'll beat what he usually gets." I replied, but my laugh was hollow and I turned my head quickly so as not to let Jess see that I was crying. Futile, really, as of course she knew I was crying! She knew me better than most people did!

Another surprise awaited when we took the horses back to the yard after a short ride. A strange man was there and I naturally assumed him to be the new owner. He appeared to be deep in conversation with Roger Brookes and I assumed they were talking over the final details of the sale now. They would be arranging the details of when my dream horse would be driven straight through the gates for the final time and there was not one single thing I could do to stop it from happening. Just like Beauty, just like Heidi.

"Anyway" the man was saying, " Nice talking to you, but I wanted to ask you about the chestnut gelding, I take it this is him? I might be interested in buying him but obviously you'd have to let me try him first."

"I'm very sorry" said Roger Brookes, thrusting his hands deeply into his jacket pockets, "You're just a bit too late. He's no longer for sale. But I'll get back to you if any jobs come up at the haulage yard, OK?"

"OK, and thanks, it was just on the off chance. Should have got your number and given you a call, but I was passing this way anyway. There's someone down at Bank End got a mare for sale, might be lucky there." The man smiled at us all and went back to his car. Nothing more remained for me to do but unsaddle Barney and put him in his stable for what may well be the last time, as it would no longer be his stable. It would lie empty until a strange, new horse arrived and I would have to get to know him or her, and maybe even fall in love again and go through all this pain...again. I knew I was being melodramatic but I couldn't help it now. It was now the third time in quite rapid succession that I'd been in this situation. First Beauty, then Heidi and now Barney. All ideal horses for me, but all now gone or almost gone.

"I just hope Barney's new owner is someone who's going to love him and take care of him, it's what he deserves!" I said to Jess as I struggled to hang up the heavy saddle, probably for the final time. I looked at Jess, pretending to be cool and calm and over it….then I burst into tears.

"It's OK" said Jess, "Don't worry about Barney's new owner. I knew you'd feel like this so Dad and I have come up with something. It'll hopefully go some way to making up for this. I hope you'll like it." Her tone betrayed nothing but I knew they felt sorry for me and I felt wretched. Platitudes or the most beautiful book or horse statue in the world would be a nice gesture but it would not fill the looming flame-coloured gap which was Barney…

"I think you should come into the house, Helen, and we'll have a talk about this." My legs could hardly carry me to the house. Once again I looked around enviously at their living room, at the immaculate carpet, the tasteful paintings adorning the walls and the classy statues and ornaments on their dust-free mantle. Their living room lacked the damp stains and badly disguised marks of cat and dog sick on our threadbare carpet, as we could neither afford to get it cleaned or get a new one. None of that mattered now. I would have starved or lived in a hut for the rest of my life if I could only have the horse of my dreams.

I was puzzled and even slightly dizzy as my head swam with emotions and my stomach lurched. I had to steady myself as I was not expecting this at all and in my daze had no idea why I was here and what any of it meant. Once Barney had gone to his new home, I was supposed to be very happy for him but I just could not bear the thought of never, ever seeing him again. I supposed, sadly, that I would eventually get used to the sick, empty feeling and it would turn to numbness over time, but recovery from this was still a long way off for now.

"We've been talking" said Roger Brookes, and Jess's mother was in the room too, all of them looking very serious indeed. "You two girls have been through a hard time just recently, but especially you, Helen. Not only did you have to endure that mugging, but before that you lost Heidi and then you found out what Derek really was. And now finding out that Barney's to go as well. We want to make it up to you for being such a good friend to Jess. You do so much for us too, you've helped so much bringing on horses like Beauty, Heidi and now Barney. So we thought we'd give you a token of our appreciation." He was smiling but I was not.

"Here you go, Helen" said Jess, and she promptly handed me a small, gift-wrapped object. It was smooth and flat, very light and rectangular in shape.

Mr and Mrs Brookes did not move as they clearly wanted to see my reaction to this gift. Whatever it was, it would never make up for the loss of Barney.

My hands trembled so much that I could hardly get the wrapping off and I swallowed the lump in my throat, took a deep breath and finally removed the present from its wrapping. A blank piece of wood...then, still shaking, I turned it over. It was a wooden name plate and the name carved on it in majestic, curly lettering was "Barney."

I was trembling now. It was Barney's name plate, and I had never seen it before. He had a temporary sticker on his door and that had been removed. I didn't understand...

"You see, Helen, there's only one owner for Barney." said Roger Brookes calmly, " Only one person who can handle him and really give him all the care he needs. He's not for sale because we're not selling him on. We've decided to keep him. We've seen you bring on so many horses and work so hard only to see them go, but not this one. He's special. Barney *does* have a new owner, Helen. His new owner is you!"

I stood and gazed over the gate the following morning, my hair plastered to my face and the autumn rain pouring down on me, but I didn't care. The horses grazed in the distance, including Barney. It was a scene of peace and quiet. Of course it was not all a fairytale. Barney would remain at the

Brookes' stables but on the condition that I was responsible for his care and exercise. With his obvious jumping talent, we could work on that and start taking him to shows to see if we could make an impression. My parents backed the idea as long as I was sensible with my studies and balanced everything out. They had promised to contribute whenever possible as long as I did my share. I assured them I would, and felt so much happier than I had in a long time. Jess and I were as close as we had ever been, and in a crazy way the assault had made that happen.

My parents, meanwhile, had become friendly with Terry and it was common knowledge that they were getting a few free rides from him when the ancient Ford Cortina broke down, which was fairly often these days. He was quite often over at our house for dinner, to spare him from his mother's soggy baked beans and mash! Mum had taken quite a shine to him and even joked about him being her "toy boy."

And, as someone once said, sometimes all you want, all you're ever looking for has always been right there in front of you.

THE END

TO BE CONTINUED...

www.ingramcontent.com/pod-product-compliance
Lightning Source LLC
LaVergne TN
LVHW091103150826
845673LV00002B/706

* 9 7 9 8 6 6 0 0 4 0 2 3 8 *